FIREBASE SEVEN

ERIC S. BROWN

SEVERED PRESS
HOBART TASMANIA

FIREBASE SEVEN

PROLOGUE

Tae Phong was just another farming village . . . or rather it had been. The entire place was in ruins. Bodies of the dead lay rotting in the grass between and around the few mud brick, thatched straw roofed homes that were still standing. Private Thomas had seen some messed up stuff since arriving in Nam but this crap here. . . it was just weird. None of the bodies on the ground looked to have bullet wounds. They didn't show signs of torture either. Most of them were crushed, the white of broken bones protruding through ruptured flesh.

"What the hell, man?" Hollen whispered, standing next to him with his M-60 hefted into a firing position. Thomas swallowed hard, trying to keep his fear in check, and motioned for Hollen to shut up.

The rest of their squad was spread out, some watching the trees, other wandering about the village looking at the dead. Captain Whedon was kneeling over the top half of a dead man whose eyes were locked forever in an expression of utter terror and pain.

They had set out from Firebase Seven a few hours back. Captain Whedon hadn't told them anything about where they were headed or why. He had just ordered them to arm up and make sure to bring along two of the base's M-60s. The captain insisted they bring an M72 too. The light anti-tank weapon was strapped to Thomas' back. If it took a round from enemy fire, Thomas knew there wouldn't be much left of him yet the rocket launcher brought him some degree of comfort. It packed one hell of a punch and this was far from the first time he had carried an M72.

Thomas walked over to where Captain Whedon was. "This wasn't an attack by the N.V.A., sir."

"I know that, Private," the captain snapped, making Thomas regret opening his mouth.

"I don't see a single shell casing in the grass anywhere. And those houses. . ." Hollen said, joining the two of them.

"This wasn't a battle, boys. It was a massacre," Captain Whedon told them. He stood up and gestured down at the body in front of him.

Thomas took a closer look at the man's remains. The lower half of his body was simply gone as if something had bitten him in two and swallowed it.   Strands of red slicked, purple intestines spilled out of the man lying in the grass, already swollen from the heat of the jungle. Thomas felt bile rising in his throat. He fought it down and turned his eyes back on Captain Whedon.

"You know what did this, don't you, sir?" Thomas asked.

Captain Whedon didn't answer his question. Instead, he said, "These people weren't killed that long ago. The thing that did this could still be close by."

"What do you mean, thing?" Hollen spat out a mouthful of tobacco juice. "What? Are you saying some kind of monster did this?"

"That's one way to put it," Captain Whedon nodded.

Hollen laughed but Thomas could tell that the captain was deadly serious.

"Captain!" Specialist Davis cried out from somewhere at the northern end of the village. Their squad had entered the village from the south. "You gotta see this, sir!"

Whedon, Hollen, and Thomas jogged over to Davis' position to see what he had found. Davis stood before a path that had been ripped through the jungle as if a tank had rolled through it. The path was wider than the width of a tank though and there were no tread tracks in the ground. If anything, the soft dirt appeared to have been pushed flat and smoothed down. The trees were knocked over and crushed. Thomas stared at the path torn into the jungle in utter shock and disbelief. He'd never seen anything like it.

"Frag me," Hollen muttered, his voice no louder than a whisper.

"What do you reckon did that, Cap?" Davis asked. "Sure as hell wasn't no tank. Look at the ground."

Before anyone could answer Davis, all hell broke loose on the other side of the village. The sound of snapping trees cracked in the night. Captain Whedon could hear the men of the fireteam that had been on that side of the village screaming in terror. Gunfire intermingled with their cries as they opened fire into the trees. Captain Whedon, Hollen, and Thomas were still sprinting towards them when the gigantic monster the fireteam was targeting came bursting out of the jungle. Its huge yellow eyes burnt like fires hovering in the darkness high above the ground.

Captain Whedon skidded to a stop, staring at the monster. The thing was impossibly fast for something its size. The snake's body curved and zagged as it rushed forward and struck at the closest of his men. Private Bryson was swallowed whole by the massive snake in a single upwards flick of its head. M14 and M1 Garand rounds hammered into the creature's sides. Most of them appeared to strike the snake's scales only to spark against them and bounce harmlessly away. The few that pierced the giant snake's body didn't have any discernable effect on the monster. The snake was too large for Captain Whedon's mind to really process. It had to be hundreds of feet long. The snake hissed as its head rose up, its yellow eyes blazing with anger.

"Run!" someone shouted. Captain Whedon understood their fear but running wasn't an option. If the giant snake wanted them dead, they would be. The best option was to do what they had come to do which was kill the fragging thing.

"Screw that," Thomas growled through clenched teeth. He was terrified but knew that running was suicide. Thomas dropped his rifle and swung the M72 L.A.W. off his back into his hands. Rifles from the spread out members of the squad were still barking, booming, hosing the giant snake with rounds as Thomas yanked the L.A.W. into being full extended. He shouldered the weapon, taking aim at the snake. The creature had swallowed another soldier whole and changed the course of its charge. Private Dax died as the thing slithered over him. His body was crushed to a pulp beneath the massive weight of the snake. Thomas lost sight of the snake's head. It was far past his position now. He watched the moonlight gleaming off the rippling scales of its side as the snake's long body kept moving by him. Thomas fired the M72. A light ant-tank round struck the snake, detonating, to blow a man-sized hole in through its scales. Bright red blood splashed outward from the wound. It rained over Thomas where he stood. Thomas cast aside his empty M72, snatching his rifle back up from where he had discarded it.

The snake stopped its forward motion as its tail whipped about in pain and rage. Hollen tried to dodge as it slashed through the air in his direction. There was just no way to escape something that large and close to the ground though. It smashed into Hollen, caving in his ribcage and snapping his arms. The white of broken bone pierced the flesh of both of his elbows where he had jerked up his arms in an attempt to protect himself. His corpse went flying through the air to go bouncing across the muddy ground of the village, landing over a dozen yards away from where he had been standing.

As the snake surged forward again, blood leaking from the hole the anti-tank had torn in its side, Private Clayton came into view. He was carrying one of the squad's M-60s. Clayton leveled the barrel of the heavy gun towards the snake and started shooting from the hip. The M-60 roared, spent round casings flying, as Clayton poured fire into the monster. The high-powered bullets ripped a swath of splattering red up the snake's side and along its back. Clayton was screaming a battle cry as he held the M-60's trigger tight.

Captain Whedon watched the snake tear into the jungle, knocking over and uprooting trees from the muddy earth. His men had managed to hurt the monster. At least he hoped that was true. They had made the thing bleed. The giant snake vanished in the darkness of the jungle. Its blazing yellow eyes gone from sight. He could still hear the creature though and knew the thing was still close by.

Private Thomas ran up next to Captain Whedon.

"Hollen's dead, sir," Thomas said.

"Look around, kid," Captain Whedon told him. "We lost a lot more than just Hollen."

Thomas saw that the captain was right. There were only four members of the squad left who weren't wounded, dead, or in the snake's stomach - himself, Merrick, Captain Whedon, and Clayton. The snake had crushed other members of the squad by wrapping them up in its body as it moved, twisting around them. Private Adams lay a few feet away from where Thomas was standing. Adams' body was crumpled up and half buried in the mud of the wet earth. He had been completely crushed by the giant snake. Even his eyeballs had popped from their sockets from the strength of the pressure the snake had gripped with him before releasing him as it slithered on over his corpse. The eyeballs dangled on the cheeks of Adams' collapsed skull, held there by thin strands of sinew. Thomas lost it at the sight of Adams. He fell to his knees, vomiting.

"Get it together," Captain Whedon barked, grabbing Thomas and yanking him back up onto his feet. "That thing ain't gone."

"Sir!" Clayton called out to Whedon, pointing into the trees. "That thing is turning around!"

Thomas watched Captain Whedon's head jerk around as if he were looking for something. Captain Whedon spotted the squad's other M-60 beside the corpse of the soldier who had been carrying it. He sprinted towards it, sweeping the heavy weapon up into his hands. Quickly checking to make sure everything was okay with the feed of its ammo belt and that the M-60 wasn't jammed, Captain Whedon took up a firing position, side by side with Clayton.

Thomas saw a shotgun lying nearby. He tossed aside his rifle and rushed to pick it up. The M870 shotgun was likely to do more damage to the snake or so he figured. . . not that Thomas really thought anything was going to stop the giant snake. It had survived the entire squad shooting the hell out of it and a direct hit to its side by an L.A.W too. Thomas' hands were shaking as he readied the shotgun.

"Here it comes!" Clayton yelled.

Trees toppled, their trunks cracking and snapping, as the giant snake came charging through them back towards the village. Its yellow eyes were locked onto the three of them. The snake was smart enough to keep its mouth shut so they couldn't fire directly into it.

"Give it hell!" Captain Whedon shouted as his finger tightened on the trigger of his M-60. Both he and Private Clayton let loose on the monster. The giant snake veered away from the trio of soldiers to protect its face and head from being torn up by the bullets they were pouring into it. The heavy M-60 rounds gouged into the snake's side, riddling the areas where they struck it with bloody holes. The problem was that the snake was so massive that even rounds high powered enough to penetrate its scales could only do so much damage. The giant snake curved around suddenly, striking with blinding speed. It snatched Clayton up in its mouth. One of the snake's fangs impaled him, sinking through his chest and out his back. The creature's mouth closed on him. The full strength of its jaws came down on Clayton's body with a sick crunching noise as his bones were crushed inside of him. Instead of trying to swallow Clayton, the snake flung away his corpse, rearing back its head to strike again at Captain Whedon.

Captain Whedon held his ground, determined to go out fighting and to take the giant snake to hell with him if he could. His M-60 continued to blaze away at the monster as its head streaked towards him. Heavy rounds dug into the soft flesh of the snake's exposed inner mouth. At the last possible moment, Merrick leaped at him, shoving Captain Whedon aside. Merrick looked up in the burning eyes of the giant snake. Its mouth envelopded him as he was swept upwards from the ground. All that Thomas could see of Merrick was a fleeting glimpse of his feet protruding from the snake's mouth before the thing's throat muscles pulled them inside of it too.

The barrel of Thomas' shotgun flashed as the weapon thundered. He had aimed for the underside of the snake's throat. The slug from the weapon hit exactly where he intended, blowing a chunk of bloody scales off the monster's body but Thomas couldn't tell if the snake even felt the shot. The snake coiled itself up, head ducked behind a thick wall of its own body. Thomas knew it was getting ready to strike at them. Captain Whedon and Clayton continued to bloody the snake, concentrating their fire together to make as large of a wound as they could.

The snake's head rose up above its coiled body. It snapped out at the captain and Clayton. Captain Whedon tried to throw himself flat but wasn't fast enough. The snake's mouth took his head from his shoulders. Blood exploded out of the mangled top of his neck. Clayton avoided being caught by the snake's wide maw altogether but didn't escape being injured. As the giant snake's head withdrew, it bumped him with enough force to shatter his right arm above his elbow and sent him reeling sideways. Clayton's M-60 splashed into the mud, too heavy for him to retain his grip on with only one hand as he struggled to stay on his feet. Thomas rushed forward, taking a shot at the snake's head as it withdrew but tripped over Captain Whedon's twiching corpse which had collapsed into his path. His shotgun boomed as he squeezed its trigger, the blast still managing to graze the edge of the giant creature's neck. The snake's head jerked back around, its yellow eyes burning, bright and hot, with primal fury. It was in no position to make another strike at him so the snake instead took a swipe at Thomas with its tail. Clayton was between him and the tail though. It caught Clayton dead on, shattering the bones of his upper body, lifting him off the ground. Clayton's corpse went hurling through the air above as Thomas scrambled to keep from being struck the snake's tail too. He splashed into the mud, the tail slashing over him. As soon as it had passed him, Thomas was crawling forward, trying to shove himself back onto his feet. He made it, breaking into a run, as the snake's tail came sweeping backwards at him again. This time there was no avoiding it. The massive tail slammed into him. Thomas' body flattened against it from the force with which it struck him. His spine broke, neck snapped, and pelvis shattered. Blood exploded out of his mouth in a spray of red. The tail swept him into the trunk of a tree, splattering Thomas' body over it in a second explosion of blood and gore.

FIREBASE SEVEN

Higman cranked up the music as the Huey flew through the air above the dense jungle below. Eric Burdon's voice belted out the lyrics of 'We Gotta Get Out of This Place' as the copter zigged to the right for no apparent reason. Clark was the sort of pilot who liked to keep everyone awake and on edge. . . as if they weren't enough already.

"What the hell was that about?" Keaton barked at Clark.

With a wry grin, Clark turned his head to say, "Just some turbulence, sir."

"Right," Keaton growled, knowing full well it hadn't been. If Clark's showing off was the worst thing he had to deal with today, Keaton figured he could take it in his stride and not shoot the A hole in the back of his head. Cassaday, the co-pilot of the Huey, was a dependable guy. Keaton knew

Cassaday wouldn't let Clark get too out of control. They all knew an RPG could come streaking up out of the jungle at them at any second. The NVA was supposed to be up to something big in this region. At least that's what Keaton had heard anyway. Regardless, he and his men had their own ballgame to deal with. They were headed to Firebase Seven. The base was way the frag out in the middle of nowhere. Its location was about as important to the war as the crap he had taken this morning. The reports Keaton had read about the place said it was undermanned and home to troopers that the brass deemed to be a waste of a uniform. The recent activity around it by the NVA and the reports coming in from its C.O., Captain Whedon, had drawn the attention of the brass back to it though. Villages near Firebase Seven had been entirely wiped out according to Whedon. . . but then other than the press and the protesters back home, who the frag cared about something like that in this war? Keaton had a difficult time figuring out why, based on what he had read and heard, the brass cared so much about whatever was going on at Firebase Seven. There had to be something more to it all but then that wasn't his job. He wasn't supposed to be taking over from Captain Whedon either which was also odd. His role in this whacked out ballgame was merely to see that Damon and his crew reached the firebase and to give them whatever support he could.

Damon and his boys had the stink of C.I.A. but they sure as hell weren't suits or pencil pushers. All three of them looked as hard as guys who had been in Nam since the war started. They shared the limited space inside the Huey with his own men. Keaton's squad consisted of two fireteams that he had hand-picked from among the best of the 75th. Sergeant Stevenson and Keaton went way back. Having Stevenson as his second in this ballgame made Keaton feel better about whatever crap they were heading into. Green, Nicholson, and Page made up the rest of Stevenson's primary fireteam. The other team consisted of Boone, Collins, Pressley, and Langley.

Hyatt, the copter's door gunner, sat at his post, one hand resting atop the M-60 pointed at the ground below. In his other hand was a cigarette. Hyatt took a long drag off of it as Captain Keaton watched him. Door gunners didn't live long. It was a suck job. Hyatt's eyes were on the jungle below. There was a hunger in them that made Captain Keaton look away. He turned his gaze to look out the window next to him on the other side of the copter. They had to be getting close to Firebase Seven. Captain Keaton lit up his own cigarette. The day was hot as hell. Sweat slicked his skin beneath his clothes. Captain Keaton's M-16 was propped against his seat between his legs. Wiping at the sweat on his brow with the backside of his hand, Captain Keaton frowned as Firebase

Seven came into view.

Firebase Seven was dug out atop a small hill. There were copter landing areas on both of its far sides. It had been built as a temporary encampment that had become a much more permanent one for the men stationed there. The base's battery of six 155mm howitzers were spread out behind the thick berms of dirt that served as its protective walls. A barbed wire fence that looked to have been hastily erected also surrounded areas of the firebase. One the howitzers sat directly in the base's center so that it could fire illumination during any attacks that came under the cover of night and also to serve as the main registration gun. The other howitzers were laid out in a star pattern in terms of their placement.

The base had four makeshift buildings within it. One was its tactical operations center which sat next to what looked to be the base's communications bunker. On its other side was a small structure that was clearly the base's aid station. A flag bearing a red cross blew in the wind outside of it. Scattered around and between the buildings were masses of tents where soldiers were busy going about their daily routines though some of them had stopped and stood watching their Huey approach. On the western side of the base, an M48 tank was parked. There was a black painted gun truck amid the Jeeps parked on the eastern side of the firebase.

Clark brought the copter down in the landing area on the southern side of Firebase Seven which was closer to the T.O.C. as Captain Keaton thought about just how understrength the place had looked to be as they had flown over it. Usually a base like this one had an entire company of infantry assigned to it. If he remembered what he had read correctly, Firebase Seven was home to only fifty or so soldiers under Captain Whedon's command. Random guerilla attacks by the NVA and simple attrition had taken their toll on the base's personnel, wearing them down to those that remained now.

Sergeant Stevenson leaped out of the Huey, waving everyone else out behind him. Damon lingered for a second, the two of them exchanging a look that Captain Keaton figured was meant to remind him exactly who was in command of this op. Then Damon followed the others out.

Captain Keaton slapped a hand on Cassady's shoulder where the man sat in the Huey's co-pilot seat. "Thanks for the ride."

Clark heard him and laughed. "Just doing our patriotic duty, man!"

"Watch yourself out, sir," Cassady added.

"You too," Captain Keaton told them both and then turned and left the Huey, hopping out onto the dirt of the landing area.

A thick muscled man with a red beard and the rank of sergeant on his sleeve came out of the

T.O.C. to meet them. Captain Keaton knew Damon wasn't going to deal with the man. That was his job.

The sergeant came to an abrupt halt in front of him, belting out, "Welcome to Firebase Seven, sir!"

Captain Keaton glanced over his shoulder, watching the Huey return to the sky. It lifted off and flew away from the firebase.

"I'm getting too old for this crap," Keaton muttered under his breath.

"Sir?" the redheaded sergeant said.

"What's your name, Sergeant?" Captain Keaton asked.

"Folks just call me Red, sir," the sergeant answered.

Keaton grunted. "And where is Captain Whedon?"

"Uh. . . he's not here, sir," Sergeant Red shrugged. "He led a squad into the jungle last night, sir."

"What?" Captain Keation actually took a step forward without meaning to.

"Captain Whedon said he had figured out what was wiping the countryside out there clean of people and that he was going to deal with it and get proof before you arrived," Sergeant Red stammered.

"And he hasn't come back yet?" Captain Keaton frowned.

"No, sir," Sergeant Red shook his head in the negative. "Haven't been able to raise him on the radio either."

Captain Keaton sighed. "Fine. You're the ranking officer here now, aren't you?"

"No, sir. That would be Lieutenant Fogerty, sir," Sergeant Red informed him.

"And he's inside there?" Captain Keaton gestured at the T.O.C.

"Yes sir," Sergeant Red's head bobbed up and down.

"I will be officially assuming command of this firebase, Sergeant, after I talk with him. Do you have any issue with that?" Keaton stared at the hulking redhead. Loyalty was a tricky thing this deep in the jungle. Captain Keaton had no desire to be woken up by a grenade being rolled into his tent. It was best to get things sorted from the get go and know where everyone stood.

"No, sir!" Sergeant Red barked.

Captain Keaton smiled at Red's answer and started walking on past the sergeant toward the tactical command center.

Sergeant Stevenson stepped up taking over things with Sergeant Red. He would handle getting the men settled into their new homes at the firebase. Captain Keaton saw that Damon had been closely watching his entire exchange with the redheaded sergeant. Things had gone badly enough even without the C.I.A. operative butting in. Keaton couldn't prove that Damon was C.I.A. Even if he wasn't though, Keaton would bet his balls that Damon was working for them.

Damon motioned for his men to accompany Captain Keaton's and then followed him on into the T.O.C. It was empty except for a single young soldier who was reading through a stack of papers. He sat at the large table in the center of the T.O.C. There was a map of the area unrolled and tacked down atop it. The young soldier saw them enter and leaped to his feet, standing at attention.

"At ease, Lieutenant," Captain Keaton waved for him to sit back down. "I'm Captain Daniel Keaton and this is . . . exactly what the hell are you again, Damon?"

Damon grinned. "You can call me Chief."

"Ha. Sure thing. As I was saying, this is Chief Damon," Captain Keaton continued. "We're here because of whatever crap's been going on that has your captain freaking out."

"Sir, yes sir," Lieutenant Fogerty snapped.

"What part of at ease did you not understand, young man?" Captain Keaton glared at the young lieutenant.

"Sorry, sir," Lieutenant Fogerty said.

"Now would you like to tell me why this firebase's commanding officer took a squad into the jungle when he knew we were expected to arrive today?" Captain Keaton challenged him.

Lieutenant Fogerty looked nervous as he

answered, "Captain Whedon. . .sir. . .he was determined to stop the slaughter of the native folk in this area. Said he couldn't just sit by and watch them get wiped out."

"That wasn't his job here," Damon huffed.

"He was well aware of that. . .uh. . . sir," Lieutenant Fogerty seemed unsure how to properly address the black clad soldier. Damon's uniform was unlike any used by the army in Nam. It was jet black and laced with some sort of lightweight, underlying armor in certain areas where it covered his chest and arms. . He was carrying a clearly modified M-16A1.

"Then what the hell is he up to, Lieutenant?" Captain Keaton snapped, calling the young man's attention back to him.

"Captain Whedon had been mapping the areas where the natives claimed most of the deaths among their people were occurring from close to the time when the attacks on the villages in the region began. He wanted to find whatever was killing them and deal with it ASAP. From what he said, the captain thought he finally had a chance of coming face to face with whatever is out there last night. That's why he took two fireteams and headed out," Lieutenant Forgerty paused, taking a breath, then continued, "With all due respect, Captain Keaton, he didn't believe that the brass would do anything more than send someone to replace him here."

"I see." Captain Keaton glanced over at Damon.

"You are here to replace him, aren't you sir?" the young lieutenant asked.

"Only for the time being," Captain Keaton admitted. "But you're correct. As of now, I will be assuming command here."

"Yes sir," Lieutenant Fogerty nodded.

"As I understand things, you've had no radio contact with Captain Whedon and his squad since sometime last night. Your Sergeant, Red, told us that Whedon wanted to get proof of what was happening out there in the jungle. I noticed too that you haven't mentioned the N.V.A. at all. Exactly what did your captain think he was dealing with?" Captain Keaton pressed the young lieutenant.

Lieutenant Fogerty shifted nervously. "Uh. . .well. . ."

"Go on, kid. Spit it out," Damon urged.

"The captain first noticed something strange was going on a few weeks back. Some of the villagers actually came to ask for his help. People were disappearing. Captain Whedon knew something had to be going on because the villagers usually do their best to stay away from us here. They claimed an ancient and evil Naga had been awakened by the war. . . that it was devouring their people. Captain Whedon didn't honestly know what to make of that. He wasn't a superstitious sort of guy by nature. Hell, I'm not even sure he believed in God, ya know? Still, Captain Whedon didn't feel like he could just sit back and do nothing. He increased our patrols," Lieutenant Fogerty was still going on but Captain Keaton interrupted him.

"And there was no sign of the N.V.A. out there?" Keaton frowned. "I was told there was increased activity in this region."

Lieutenant Fogerty shrugged. "I can't speak to what you were told, sir. What I can tell you is that there hasn't been any real change in terms of the N.V.A. here. Our patrols still encounter them from time to time. Skirmishes happen but there's no sign of them massing forces out there or of any kind of coming attack on this base by them."

Captain Keaton shook his head in frustration.

"Anyway. . ." Lieutenant Fogerty continued. "What we did find out there was. . .I guess you'd call it a shrine. That's what the captain called it anyway. Finding places like it in these jungles isn't something that's too out of place but. . . this one. . . it weighed on the captain. Like he couldn't let it go. The shrine was torn up pretty bad. The captain thought maybe an artillery shell had hit it. Even as blown apart as the place was, he said it looked as if some of the villagers were still worshipping this Naga they had come to him about there or at least leaving the thing offerings. Makes sense. If you think that way, trying to buy the

Naga off with offerings to keep it from killing you and yours makes sense."

"Are you getting around to saying that Captain Whedon believed the Naga was real?" Damon asked.

"Whoa," Captain Keaton held up a hand. "One of you want to tell me exactly what a fragging Naga is?"

"A Naga is a god or demi god related to serpents. There are a lot of faiths in this region of the world that Naga are a part of. Usually a Naga is described as a half snake, half human being but not always. A Naga can also just be a snake. However, in the bulk of stories and legends about Naga, they are not evil. It's mostly in western culture that considers serpents to be creatures of evil," Damon filled him in.

"Captain Whedon believed this one was," Lieutenant Fogerty sighed. "He thought it was a local god."

"Then he did believe this Naga thing was real?" Captain Keaton pressed.

"Like I said, Captain Whedon wasn't big on the supernatural stuff but he did believe something was out there," Lieutenant Fogerty shrugged.

"What does that even mean?" Captain Keaton scowled, reaching into the pocket of his shirt to retrieve the pack of cigarettes there. He took one out and lit it up.

"He thought there was a monster in the

jungle," Damon said.

Lieutenant Fogerty nodded. "That's the best way to put it, I guess. That there was something out there that couldn't be explained, something that was killing the villagers, and whatever it was, Captain Whedon wanted to see it dead."

"What a mess," Damon muttered so quietly that Captain Keaton barely heard him.

"And that's why he took out a squad last night? He was going after this monster?" Captain Keaton stared at Lieutenant Fogerty.

"Yes sir," the young lieutenant answered.

"You said there wasn't a build or surge in the N.V.A. activity here," Damon spoke up. "But I get the feeling that there's something you're leaving out."

"I told you they are still leaving us alone for the most part other than the usual skirmishes in the jungle," Lieutenant Fogerty responded.

"But. . ." Damon challenged him.

"But one of our patrols did run into something odd. On a road to the north of here, they found a convoy of N.V.A. trucks. Apparently the N.V.A. were trying to bring more troops into the region quickly. Something, likely the same thing that's been wiping out the villages, met up with them. The trucks were messed up bad. They were all rolled over onto their sides or turned over completely. Some of them were, for lack of a better word, crushed. Like something had plowed over the top of them. There was one that looked like it had been put in a wringer. That one was just a mass of twisted up metal sitting there in the middle of the road with congealed blood covering it. That worried Captain Whedon a lot though you think he would have been happy to hear about the N.V.A. being hit like that. Deep down, I am sure a part of him was," Lieutenant Fogerty moved to point at a spot on the map which was rolled out atop the table. "We found those trucks right about here."

Damon grunted. The location of the road was a good distance away from Firebase Seven.

"Is that where Captain Whedon headed last night?" Captain Keaton asked.

"No, sir," Lieutenant Fogerty moved his finger across the map. "He was headed here to Tae Phong. It's the last village left in this area. Captain Whedon was sure that whatever is out there would be hitting it last night. That's why he left. He wanted to be there when Tae Phong got hit. Captain Whedon hoped he could stop the Naga or whatever and if he couldn't that he could at least get proof enough of the thing to convince you that it was real when you arrived."

"Idiot," Damon growled.

Captain Keaton's head whipped around at the C.I.A. operative. "Is there something you'd like to share with us, Chief?"

Damon glared at him. Technically Damon

outranked him in this ballgame. Captain Keaton's job was to support him and his men in whatever they were up to. . . but whatever it was, it was classified. He left Damon with no choice but to defer to him in front of the young lieutenant.

"No, sir," Damon answered. Captain Keaton figured he was going to pay for what he had just done later on.

"Okay then," Captain Keaton nodded. "Lieutenant, I want all of your captain's papers and notes ready for me to browse through within the hour. We'll take things from there and see what our next course of action will be. That will give Captain Whedon a bit longer to check in though I think it's safe to say that he has run into some kind of trouble at this point and we can't count on that."

Damon left the T.O.C. without looking back, leaving Captain Keaton to deal with things which needed to be attended to in terms of Firebase Seven and its personnel.

****

Haley and Berrong were on watch as the helicopter flew in, dropped off whoever was on it, and left as quickly as it had come. Berrong was puffing on a cigarette and scowling as they both stared into the brush of the jungle beyond the perimeter of Firebase Seven.

"That ain't good," Berrong commented in the

wake of the copter's departure.

Haley shook his head and sighed. "Don't mean nothing."

"Oh yeah it does," Berrong grumbled. "It means Whedon couldn't handle things out here and now who knows what kind of new prick C.O. we're going to be saddled with."

"You really have a way of always looking on the bright side of things, don't you?" Haley quipped.

"Like you got room to talk," Berrong shot back at him.

"Hey," Haley argued, "I just call them as I see them."

"Sure," Berrong snorted.

"Anyway, who's to say that we're getting a new C.O., man? Could be just some temp. support ya know, until we get things sorted out," Haley suggested.

"Whedon's done and fragged up bad, buddy and you know it," Berrong laughed.

Haley cocked an eyebrow at Berrong. He wanted to stand up for the captain but knew Berrong was right. Whedon had totally gone off into the deep end of late. The guy really thought that there was some sort of monster out there in the jungle. There were plenty of monsters as far as Haley was concerned but they were men carrying AK-47s who were out for their blood, not whatever the hell the captain had been on about.

Haley was dang glad Whedon hadn't picked him for the squad he'd led out last night. Something in Haley's gut told him that none of those guys would ever be coming back or the captain either. He kept that to himself though.

"Still, things could be worse," Haley shrugged.

Their relief showed up to take their place as Haley and Berrong's turn on watch ended. They headed back into the firebase, glad to be out of the foxhole they'd been in. Berrong lit up another cigarette as they walked towards the firebase's makeshift mess tent. Haley's stomach was rumbling. The smell coming out of the mess tent made Haley wriggle his nose despite his hunger. Another big, ole round of beef stew was on the menu again this afternoon. The thought of it nearly turned his stomach but Haley knew he was hungry enough to eat pretty much anything that Cookie slopped out on his plate.

Haley and Berrong paused just short of the mess tent's entrance. They saw a group of new faces in the camp, all with plates of grub, sitting outside the firebase's barracks.

"What the hell?" Berrong wondered aloud. "I didn't know we were getting reinforcements?"

"You just said a few minutes ago that you thought the copter was bringing in support for us," Haley reminded him.

"Yeah, but I was just mouthing off. I thought

we'd get a new C.O. with an aide or two, not a brand new freaking squad," Berrong snapped.

"More than just a squad," Haley nodded at the three men who were sitting apart from the rest of the new faces. "Who do you think they are?"

"Nobody good." Berrong had an expression of disgust on his face. "Look at them. What the hell is that crap they're wearing? They ain't regular army, I'll tell you that."

Haley could see that for himself. The three guys were wearing black flak jackets but that wasn't all. They were decked out head to toe, from armored pads on their elbows and knees to much tougher, better looking boots than grunts like themselves got issued. Haley whistled at the amount of firepower the three men had brought with them. All three had brand new looking M-16s that looked to have had some modifications made to them among their gear. The slender man with black hair and pale skin, who was clearly their leader, also carried a wicked looking shotgun unlike anything Haley had ever seen. Another of the three had what looked to be a scaled down version of a GAU-17/A mini-gun. And the last was packing matching UZIs. Haley wondered just who in the hell they were and why they had been sent to Firebase Seven.

He and Berrong grabbed their grub and came back out of the mess tent to try to find a spot in the shade to eat. The day was fragging hot. It felt like the temp was pushing a hundred degrees. Haley was sweating like a pig but he was used to that now. It seemed like every day was either raining or crazy hot. In truth, he preferred the rain to the heat most of the time. The air always seemed to be humid regardless.

Sergeant Red was with the new sergeant that had come in with the fresh squad of normal troops. The two of them were talking. Haley couldn't hear what about but their discussion wasn't heated. Both men appeared to be getting along with one another well enough.

"Hey!" one of the new soldiers called to them, gesturing for the two of them to join the group eating a late lunch outside the barracks.

"Thanks, man," Berrong grunted, moving to sit down next to one of the new soldiers. Haley followed him.

"You guys got names?" Haley asked the two they had sat down with.

"I'm Boone," the burly, short man next to Berrong answered, "And that's Collins."

"Chao," Collins grinned, giving them a mock salute.

"Guess you guys just got transferred here, huh?" Berrong asked.

"No, sir," Boone shook his head as if insulted and then motioned at the men in black armor. "We're just here to help out those frag heads."

"And just who the frag are they anyway?"

Berrong speared a meatball on his plate and shoveled it into his mouth.

Boone chuckled. "That's above my paygrade."

"I get the feeling it's above the captain's too," Collins added.

"Captain Whedon?" Haley asked.

"Nah, man," Boone told him. "Captain Keaton. He's our C.O. Flew in on the copter with us."

Haley and Berrong exchanged a concerned look. Collins must have noticed it.

"He ain't staying either," Collins grinned. "At least I'm pretty sure he's not."

The leader of the troopers in black left the other two where they were and headed towards the T.O.C.

"Wonder what he's up to," Haley commented.

"Your guess is as good as mine, man," Collins shrugged.

****

Captain Keaton had finished looking over Captain Whedon's reports by the time that Damon returned to the Tactical Operations Center. Things weren't good but then he had known they wouldn't be long before they arrived at Firebase Seven. And they could have been a lot worse. In terms of ammo and supplies, the firebase was fantastic. It was their lack of personnel and tactical situation that worried him. Captain Whedon had been told that there were at least fifty soldiers stationed at the base, counting the artillery staff and medics. The truth of the matter was that even counting those groups, there were less than fifty troopers. According to Lieutenant Fogerty, there was a total of forty-two present before the arrival of himself and those who came with him. If the N.V.A. did make a move against Firebase Seven, Captain Keaton had his doubts as to whether or not it could be held. Withdrawing wasn't an option though unless the brass approved the air cavalry to do it. God only knew what was lurking out there in the jungle. Captain Keaton was pretty fragging sure there wasn't a real monster out there despite what he had read in Captain Whedon's reports and what Lieutenant Fogerty had told him. This was the real world not some horror film. His orders hadn't included assuming command of the firebase, not really, he and his squad were just supposed to be support for Damon's crew. Yet he was left with no choice but to do just that.

"Where's the kid?" Damon asked upon entering the T.O.C.

"I dismissed the lieutenant a few minutes ago," Captain Keaton answered. "Figured he needed some rest. The kid has been up all night trying to contact Whedon."

"That guy was a fool," Damon commented.

"Should have waited on us to get here."

Captain Keaton cocked an eyebrow at the C.I.A. operative. "You know I think it's time you told me more about why exactly we're here."

Damon shrugged. "Think what you want."

"We have to assume that Captain Whedon and those that went out with him last night are dead," Captain Keaton frowned.

"Oh, you can bet they are," Damon agreed.

"I understand that you are not under my direct command, Damon, but the security of this base is just as important as whatever you're up to out here." Captain Keaton looked Damon in the eye as he spoke. "So let me be clear right now. I am not going to allow you to endanger this base. I'll do my job and give you the support you need but that's it. You understand me?"

"I understand you, Captain," Damon nodded. "But you need to understand that the thing out there in the jungle. . . it has to be dealt with and quickly."

"Thing?" Captain Keaton repeated the word with a wry grin on his face. "So what? Are you telling me that there's really some kind of monster or spirit out there?"

"I am saying my men and I will be heading out at first light tomorrow. I'll be taking your squad with me too," Damon's voice was cold and hard.

Captain Keaton knew he couldn't stop Damon

from doing what he said short of placing the man under arrest and that would be a violation of his orders which would likely cost lives in the process. Damon and his buddies weren't people anyone in their right mind would want to go up against. He wanted his own men at the firebase to bolster its low number of defenders should it come under attack while Damon's crew were out there chasing phantoms.

"Look," Damon suddenly shifted his tone. "I get that you weren't expecting to take over the role of C.O. here or that things would be in such a mess. Whedon screwed us both over. There's no denying that. The fool should have waited on us to get here but he didn't and now we're stuck dealing with the crap he's left us. I'm not trying to frag you over, Captain. I've just got a job to do and one that has to be done. The N.V.A. haven't made a real move against this place yet and we've got no reason to think they're about to now. . . not with the crap going on out there in the jungle around it."

"Somehow I don't find that very comforting." Captain Keaton knew Damon was right but that didn't mean he had to like it.

"Let your men know I'll need them in the morning. Have them geared up and ready to roll," Damon ordered. "Oh, and we'll be taking the gun truck too."

Captain Keaton had given up arguing with the C.I.A. man. "Fine," he growled. "Anything else?"

"Nope," Damon grinned. "But I would suggest you get some rest. Odds are you're going to need it whipping this place into shape while we're gone."

****

Sergeant Stevenson hadn't taken the news about heading out at first light very well. It fragging sucked. With the disappearance of Captain Whedon and those he had taken with him, Firebase Seven was even more unmanned than it had been and that meant someone had to pick up the slack. Sergeant Stevenson had volunteered to take a shift on watch for the night before Captain Keaton had passed on Damon's order about the next day to him. That meant he would be pulling an all-nighter right before heading out with that C.I.A. prick's crew in the jungle to God only knew where.

As the sun set and darkness fell, Sergeant Stevenson found himself in a foxhole just beyond Firebase Seven's perimeter. On the upside, it wasn't raining and Sergeant Red had volunteered to join him. It was nice to be sharing the watch with someone who had taken fire before instead of some nervous private. Red was a big guy and ate like one. As Stevenson lit up a smoke, careful to cover the glow of the match he used, Red was chowing down on a ration bar.

"It's too bad about Captain Whedon," Red commented around the mouthful he was chewing. "He was a good man."

"Good don't get you much in this war except dead, son," Stevenson said.

Red was a few years younger than he was. It seemed like most of the soldiers at Firebase Seven were youngsters to Stevenson. That was a sad thing. So many of America's youth had been drafted into service. There was a time when Stevenson truly believed in the war but now, he wasn't so sure anymore.

"You know those things are bad for you, right?" Red gestured at his cigarette.

Stevenson chuckled, ignoring the kid's question. "I hear things have been quiet here with the N.V.A."

"Oh yeah," Red smiled. "Thank God for that. With everything else going on it's a good thing too."

The moon was high in the sky above them and the night was clear. The shadows in the trees beyond where the jungle had been pushed back around the firebase were deep though. There were of course lights on inside the firebase's perimeter. Captain Keaton was likely still getting a feel of things and likely was too busy to have clamped down on any partying the previous C.O. had allowed.

"Hey!" Red slapped him on the shoulder,

pointing southward.

Stevenson looked in the direction Red had indicated but couldn't see anything except for more trees and darkness. He waited for AK-47s to open up on them from the jungle but nothing happened. The night was just as quiet and still as it had been. Red looked almost relieved and disappointed at the same time.

"Could have sworn I spotted something moving over there," Red shrugged, his wide shoulders moving up and down.

"Don't sweat it," Stevenson smiled. "Better safe than sorry. Now you want to tell me what you're doing out here?"

Red gave him a confused look.

"I can't remember the last time there were two sergeants in a foxhole like this when the crap hadn't hit the fan," Stevenson told him. "It ain't right so I have to either assume you had a reason for getting out here alone with me or you're as big of an idiot as you look like you are."

"Ya got me," Red admitted. "I do need to talk to you."

"Well best get to it then, kid," Stevenson urged. They might have the same rank but he still had seniority. "The night's a wasting."

Red took a breath and seemed to steady himself. "Do you know what Captain Whedon thought was out there attacking those villages?"

Stevenson shook his head and sighed. "Do I

even want to know?"

"The captain believed there was a monster out there. . . a dang big one too," Red said. "Like something out of a Godzilla movie."

Stevenson clapped a hand over his mouth to keep from laughing out loud. It took him a moment to see that Red honestly wasn't yanking his chain.

"Tell me you're fragging kidding," Stevenson said.

"Dead serious," Red frowned. "Captain Whedon didn't believe in the supernatural and all that stuff but he did read a lot of science fiction. You know there are a lot of biological agents being tossed about out there. It'll be a blasted miracle if we don't all go home with cancer or worse. Whedon thought maybe that crap caused some sort of mutation in the animals here or something."

"Frag. I have to admit that ain't a bad theory," Stevenson admitted, even though he didn't want to.

"That's how I saw things too," Red agreed. "Not something I like to think about given that it might be true and we're stuck out here with whatever's been messed up by the crap the bombers are dropping."

"That would explain why Damon and his crew got sent out here," Stevenson said. "If something like that had happened, you can bet the brass would want it dealt with A.S.A.P."

"You know it," Red nodded.

Stevenson finished his cigarette and leaned over where he was sitting to grind it out on the muddy ground. As he did so, a quiet gasp came from Red. Stevenson looked up to see if he was okay.

It wasn't Red he saw staring back at him though. Red's corpse lay slumped against the interior of the foxhole, his throat slashed open. Between him and Red was a creature like something straight out of hell itself. The thing in front of him was hunched over. It was roughly human shaped and likely stood around six feet tall when it was standing upright. The scales that covered its body were like those of a snake's and shaded so that the creature blended into the night around it. A forked tongue flitted in and out of its mouth as if tasting the air as it glared at him with reptilian blue eyes. The fingers of its hands were tipped with wickedly sharp looking curved claws. Stevenson managed to keep from screaming like a frightened school girl at the sight of the thing. He jerked up his rifle, aiming its barrel at the monster in the foxhole with him as its mouth opened. There was a sharp hissing noise as the creature sprayed him with something that had to be venom. It burnt like hell where it made contact with his flesh and his vision went black. Stevenson's rifle was ripped from his hands before he could squeeze its trigger. Whatever the thing was, it was fragging fast. . . faster than anything human could be. His entire world had become nothing but pain. He was blind and helpless, dying. The last thing Sergeant Stevenson felt was scaled hands take hold of the sides of his head then with a quick twist, those hands snapped his neck and it was all over.

****

"Oh frag," Lieutenant Fogerty said, looking away from what was left of Sergeant Stevenson. Fogerty dropped to his knees in the dirt of the foxhole and vomited.

Damon, Captain Keaton, and two privates from among Firebase Seven's personnel stood nearby. The two privates, Moore and Campbell, looked green too but Captain Keaton guessed they had already done their share of puking up their guts since they had been the ones to find the sergeants.

"What the frag were they both doing out here?" Captain Keaton growled but no one seemed to have an answer.

"Doesn't matter," Damon sighed. "They're dead now."

"No kidding!" Captain Keaton raged.

Sergeant Red's corpse sat on the right side of the foxhole. His back was turned to the jungle. Something had neatly opened up his neck from one shoulder to the other, slicing through his vocal chords in the process. The mess that was Sergeant

Stevenson's corpse was horrifying. The smell of it was putrid, though sweet and steaky, so powerful that Captain Keaton had gagged upon catching his first whiff of it. As bad as the smell was though, the sight of Stevenson was worse. His entire face was burnt away down to the bone as if someone had crammed it down into a vat of high-powered acid and held it there for a while. Even some of the bone was melted.

"Well that's new," Damon commented.

"Somebody get Sergeant Stevenson covered up already!" Captain Keaton barked.

Lieutenant Fogerty took off his jacket and laid it over Stevenson's corpse.

The Viet Cong were experts in coming up with terrible new means of killing U.S. Troops. Captain Keaton had seen men impaled on punji sticks with the things sticking through their guts, begging for someone to shoot them. He had seen men lose legs and their genitals to grenades in a can that lay hidden on the jungle floor until their line was tripped and they went boom. The Viet Cong also liked to bury cartridges in the dirt that would go off like a mine when they were triggered, blowing a hole in the poor bastard who stepped on it. Though he had never seen one, Captain Keaton had heard of mace traps. Spiked balls of wood or some kind of gord that would swing down and impale their victim only to then break and release trapped hornets or scorpions onto the already wounded trooper. Up until now, his own worst personal fear was the snake trap. It worked just like the punji sticks in terms of how it was concealed but when you fell into the pit, one found themselves in a mass of ticked off, poisonous snakes. Captain Keaton shuddered just at the thought of such a thing. Now though, whatever the hell they had done to Stevenson took the cake. He wasn't able to explain what the evil bastards had done to the sergeant at all.

"What the Hell?" Captain Keaton demanded. "How did they even manage this? What they did to him is insane!"

"I think the big question is who are they?" Damon said, his voice serious. The C.I.A. operative pointed at the muddy ground inside the foxhole. "An N.V.A. soldier doesn't leave footprints like these."

Captain Keaton looked down, noticing for the first time the prints in the mud. They were as large as a man's but utterly inhuman. They were deeper than a man's would be and each had three overly large toes, which based on the indentions looked to end in some kind of claw or talon. Captain Keaton blinked in shock, a gasp escaping his lips despite himself.

"Whatever left these sure as hell ain't human," Lieutenant Fogerty muttered.

Damon was looking over the whole scene. "Whatever those tracks belong to, these guys never heard it coming. That's pretty impressive considering how heavy the thing had to be in order to leave tracks as deep as these are."

"Are you saying whoever did this snuck up on them and took both of them out before either one of them could get off a single shot?" Captain Keaton stammered, still trying to get his thoughts back together and take in the madness of the tracks and what had been done to Stevenson.

"Sure looks that way, Captain," Damon nodded.

"Wait," Lieutenant Fogerty said. "If that's the case, why in the hell didn't the firebase come under attack? I mean, why did they stop here? That doesn't make any sense. They could have taken us all by surprise."

"Fogerty's right. Why stop here?" Captain Keaton turned to Damon.

"This wasn't the N.V.A. Don't you guys get that? The thing that killed these two wasn't attacking the firebase. We've got no fragging clue what its motive here was," Damon answered.

"Frag me," Lieutenant Fogerty muttered.

"I'm still taking my boys and your squad out, Captain Keaton," Damon said. "This changes nothing except that you may really want to watch your butts here while we're gone."

Captain Keaton stared at Damon, his cheeks flushed red with anger. He couldn't pull rank on Damon even if he was the firebase's new C.O.

Damon was outside of his command, not to mention both he, himself, and his squad were under orders to be support to Damon and his crew.

"Get out of my sight then," Captain Keaton growled.

Damon chuckled and headed back into Firebase Seven to get ready to roll out. "Consider me gone, Captain."

****

The Devil's Horns, Firebase Seven's resident gun truck, rolled out onto the road heading south, followed by a pair of Jeeps. Damon rode in the gun truck's cab next to Private Boone who was the truck's driver. Privates Collins, Pressley, Langley and Green rode in the rear of the truck manning its M 134 minigun which was supplemented by a pair of M-60s for support. Private Nicholson and Damon's man, Bently, rode in the first of the two Jeeps. The other was driven by Private Page with Damon's other man, Jager, riding shotgun.

The group was leaving Firebase Seven much later than Damon had intended to. The murder of the base's two sergeants during the night had set back the timetable of his plan. Damon supposed that didn't really matter but it had given him more of a chance to pick exactly where the group should head for. After re-examining the reports and logs of the base's missing C.O., he had decided the same village that Captain Whedon had set out for was the best place to start his hunt. Damon, while he had no official rank like Captain Keaton, was privy to much more information on what those stationed at Firebase Seven were up against. His superiors believed, off the record of course, that the biological agents in use against the Viet Cong were responsible for creating something terrible in this region, some sort of mutation that had become its apex predator. This creature had to be eliminated before the press got wind of it. The folks back home in the states were already turning against this war and news of their military being responsible for the creation of a monster was the last thing they needed to hear.

The village wasn't that far of a drive from the firebase. Captain Whedon had approached it during the night, hoping stealth would give him an advantage over whatever was out there. Damon's plan was rather the opposite. The five-ton gun truck and Jeeps were a show of power. He didn't want to creep up on the monster, Damon wanted to draw the thing to him. He figured that the gun truck and Jeeps would certainly get the creature's attention and hopefully make the thing feel like they were a threat to its territory. If it saw them that way, Damon knew the creature would reveal itself and come at them.

The small convoy bounced up the rough, dirt road that led into the village just as the burning sun started to descend from reaching its zenith in the sky. The heat was horrible. Damon had the gun truck's passenger side window rolled down but the heavy vehicle moved at such a slow pace there wasn't much air flowing through it into the cab to help cool its interior. Damon wiped at the sweat on his brow with the backside of his left hand.

"I think we're here, sir," Boone told him, nodding at something up ahead of the gun truck.

Damon looked out through the forward window and saw the village or rather what was left of it. Something had torn the entire place apart. The huts and houses of the people who had lived there were crushed and broken. Bodies lay rotting in the sun. The stench of the place was enough to make both of them gag even inside the gun truck. There was a deeply powerful earthy and musky edge to the smell of decay that seemed out of place and not normal. It made the hairs on Damon's neck stand up at attention though he couldn't explain why. There was nothing in sight that appeared to be a threat to him or the men he had brought with him under his command.

The gun truck rolled into the center of the village and stopped there as Boone killed its engine. The two Jeeps followed the gun truck in and parked in flanking positions near it. Damon swung the passenger door open and hopped out. As his boots hit the ground, his eyes took in his surroundings. Whatever had struck the village had hit it fast and hard. The poor bastards had never stood a chance. From the look of things, the same could be said about Captain Whedon and the men who had accompanied him. There were a few corpses dressed in U.S. Army combat uniforms. The heat and humidity had already taken its toll on them too and they were heavily decomposed. Damon dropped to one knee, looking at shell casings in the grass.

"What ya thinking, boss?" Bently asked, walking up to him.

"He's thinking we're about to get some action," Jager laughed, joining them. "Ain't that right, boss?"

Damon looked up at the two of them. "Have the men fan out and take up defensive positions. I want this place secured A.S.A.P."

"On it," Boone said and started shouting, passing on his orders to the rest of the squad.

Rolling over the shell casing he'd picked up in his fingers, Damon got to his feet. "Jager?"

Jager was the best of the best when it came to killing. That was why Damon had asked for him specifically for this op. The man was a dang skilled hunter too. If anyone knew exactly what to make of the grizzly scene around them, it would be him.

"Let me get a better look around," Jager answered.

"Go on," Damon ordered and then turned his

attention to Bently.

"Don't look too good, huh?" Bently commented. "I get that you're planning on drawing this thing, whatever it is, to us but do you really think that's a good idea, boss?"

"You got a better one?" Damon challenged him.

Bently grunted, shrugging, "Can't say that I do."

"Then shut up and stay sharp," Damon said harshly.

Bently nodded. "Will do."

"Fragging A!" one of the infantrymen from Captain Keaton's squad called out, getting everyone's attention.

Damon raced to where the soldier stood staring at the mangled trees. Something massive had ripped a trail through the jungle.

"Holy. . ." Bently breathed behind Damon.

"That's crazy," Private Green, who had been the one who called out to Damon, was still shaking his head in disbelief at the sight in front of them. "What could have done something like this?"

"Water Buffalos maybe," Bently suggested.

"Or maybe a really big tank," Private Green countered.

"When was the last time you heard of the Viet Cong fielding any kind of armor at a place as remote as this village?" Private Nicholson asked.

"No," Damon snapped. "Look at the ground.

There aren't any tracks. . . animal or machine. Everything has been flattened out as if something heavy and smooth were dragged over it."

The way the broken bits of trees were mashed down into the ground backed up what Damon was saying. Damon had never seen anything like what he was staring at before. . . the path cut through the jungle had to have been made by the creature he was after. Nothing else could have done it. Damon turned his back to the path and looked around the village again, paying more attention to the type of damage that had been inflicted upon its houses and huts. It had been clear right off that the damage wasn't caused by gunfire or grenades. Now though, Damon could almost see a pattern inside of it. If something large were moving through the village, turning and fighting, its massive body would have cut such a swath of destruction as what he was seeing.

Jager sauntered up to him. "You want the good news first or the bad?"

Damon snickered. "Does it really matter? Just get to it."

"Right," Jager nodded. "Follow me."

The professional killer led Damon back towards the center of the village where the gun truck and Jeeps were parked. He stopped, gesturing at a large patch of ground that looked to have been drenched in blood. . . a lot of fragging blood.

"I think our Captain Whedon and his squad put up one hell of a fight before whatever it is we're dealing with took them out," Jager told him. "Look at the grass and ground here."

"I see the blood," Damon assured Jager.

"Unless someone slaughtered a lot of cattle on this spot, I'd say Captain Whedon's crew got in a dang good hit or two right here," Jager said. "What's scary is knowing that whatever lost this much blood kept on, not just moving, but fighting too. Even after taking this kind of hurt, the thing clearly finished up Captain Whedon's squad afterwards."

"Any idea what this thing might be?" Damon pressed Jager.

Jager nodded, "I have an idea but you're not going to like it."

"Just spit it out," Damon ordered Jager.

"I think what we're dealing with is a bloody, fragging big snake," Jager said.

A stark chill ran through Damon and he shuddered. Why did it have to be a snake?

"Are you sure?" Damon asked.

"Pretty fragging sure," Jager nodded. "It fits with the damage around us and the two paths cut through the jungle. Must have made one on its way in and the other on its way out."

"Please tell me that was the bad news," Damon grumbled.

"Yep," Jager chuckled.

"So what's the good news then?" Damon forced himself to calm down.

"We know this thing bleeds," Jager grinned. "If it bleeds, then it can be killed."

****

The burial service for Sergeants Stevenson and Red was very brief. Their bodies were covered up with dirt inside of the foxhole where they died. Captain Keaton said some hurried words over them and that was it. He didn't mean to disrespect the dead but this was war and there were more important matters to be dealt with.

With Stevenson dead, Lieutenant Fogerty had become his new second in command. A good thing about that was the young lieutenant's knowledge of Firebase Seven, what it had on hand and was capable of, as well as his knowledge of the N.V.A. tactics in this region. The thing that killed the two sergeants clearly hadn't been human. . . at least that's what the evidence pointed to. Captain Keaton admitted to himself that he was still having a difficult time accepting that fact though. Regardless of whatever creature was out there, the Viet Cong still were too. He needed Firebase Seven to be ready for both kinds of threats before night fell. Damon taking off with his squad didn't help matters. The firebase was sorely undermanned and it would have been nice to have his own men to supplement its defense with. Sadly, that wasn't to be. There was nothing he could have legally done to stop Damon from taking them with him.

Captain Keaton had returned to the T.O.C. after the rushed burial. Damon and those with him were long gone. The sun had passed its zenith in the sky and was slowly beginning its descent. Captain Keaton worried what would be coming with the darkness. He had doubled the watch out of the men that were left under his command and put the base on alert. Those who had seen what happened to Sergeant Stevenson put the fear of God into the others. Everyone was on edge and that worked in Captain Keaton's favor. If anything tried to slink into Firebase Seven tonight, he hoped it would be met with a rain of hot lead.

Corporal Carter, who was one of the officers in charge of the firebase's howitzers, reported that all the base's weapons were in good shape and ready for action. Captain Keaton doubted any of the howitzers would be needed. They were apparently dealing with some kind of creature that quietly stalked its prey, catching them off guard, not an all-out Viet Cong attack on the base.

After thanking Carter for the good news, Captain Keaton dismissed the corporal as Lieutenant Fogerty entered the T.O.C.

"This base is as secure as it can be, sir," Lieutenant Fogerty assured him.

"Good," Captain Keaton nodded.

"It sure would be nice to know exactly what we're up against tonight," the young lieutenant commented.

Captain Keaton huffed. "I'm not sure I really want to know. I just want whatever it is dead."

"You really think we're dealing with a . . . monster?" Lieutenant Fogerty asked.

"You saw those tracks just like I did," Captain Keaton reminded him. "And there has to be something out there or the brass wouldn't have sent in Damon and his kill crew."

Captain Keaton sat behind Captain Whedon's desk. Lieutenant Fogerty took a seat in the chair that sat in front of it with a worried expression on his face.

"I hate to admit it, sir, but that makes sense," Lieutenant Fogerty frowned. "I know Captain Whedon truly believed there was something not human out there."

"I don't buy that Naga crap if that's what you're talking about," Captain Keaton snorted. "The supernatural ain't real. Whatever is out there has to be some kind of mutation caused by. . ."

Captain Keaton stared across the desk at Lieutenant Fogerty without finishing his sentence. There was no point in it. They both knew exactly what he would have said.

"I've read a lot of science fiction, sir," Lieutenant Fogerty said. "The sort of mutation you appear to be implying couldn't have happened that fast, could it?"

Shrugging, Captain Keaton answered, "I read SF too, Lieutenant. Some mutations happen faster than others. But if that's not what has happened here then I don't have a dang explanation for what's going on."

"I've been thinking about how Sergeant Stevenson died," Lieutenant Fogerty popped off. "What if it wasn't acid that melted his face?"

Leaning forward, Captain Keaton put his elbows atop the desk. "If it wasn't acid, what the hell could it have been then, Lieutenant?"

"I think it might have been venom, sir," Lieutenant Fogerty kept his voice level. "When a scorpion stings you, it hurts like hell. The thing is, I read a journal that said their venom on its own wasn't strong enough to cause that kind of pain. The guy who wrote the article claimed that the venom wasn't just a poison, it was acidic too. That's why a sting from a scorpion feels like it burns. What if this creature out there has a venom that's acidic enough to not just cause pain but melt someone's flesh like what happened to your sergeant?"

Captain Keaton cocked his head, listening to what Fogerty had to say closely. "So you think this thing, whatever it is, bit Sergeant Stevenson?"

Lieutenant Fogerty shook his head. "No, sir. I think it spat the venom on him like some types of cobras do."

"Frag," Captain Keaton muttered under his breath. "Nagas are sometimes represented in myth as cobras, aren't they?"

"I don't know about that, sir, but I do think it's something snake-like we're dealing with. Everything we've heard from the locals and what we've seen ourselves certainly point to that being the case. Don't you think so?"

Nodding, Captain Keaton opened the drawer of the desk and took out a bottle of vodka. It had belonged to the base's former C.O. who was likely dead now and had no use for it. There were shot glasses in the drawer and he got them out too, placing one in front of the young lieutenant.

"What I think, Lieutenant, is that we both need a drink," Captain Keaton said.

"No argument from me on that one, sir," Lieutenant Fogerty said, reaching for the shot glass Captain Keaton had filled up for him.

****

The shadows in the village and the jungle surrounding it were growing longer as the sun was starting to set. Damon paced back and forth in front of the gun truck. He had been so blasted sure the monster would have come for them by now. The thing had been presented with a clear threat to its territory but so far there was no sign of it.

"It'll come," Jager assured him from where he leaned against the side of the gun truck puffing on a cigarette. "Just give it time."

"Maybe the thing is scared of us," Bently snorted.

Jager glared at him. "You're a real idiot, Bently."

"Hey, a guy can hope, right?" Bently countered.

"Most likely the thing is waiting for night to fall," Jager said.

"You think it only hunts at night?" Damon questioned the lethal little man.

"No, I think it's a hell of a lot smarter than we're giving it credit for and that's what I would do in its place." Jager took a drag off his smoke.

Boone stood with the three of them, keeping his mouth shut and listening to what they were saying as closely as he could.

Page, Green, and Langley were in the rear of the gun truck manning its M 134 and M-60s. The mini-gun always reminded Boone of an old school gatling gun because of the weapon's rotating barrel assembly. The XM 134 was a hell of a sight better than any Gatling though. It could fire up to six thousand rounds a minute without overheating. The thing was just nasty. Boone was glad they had it with them based on what he was hearing too. He hadn't joined up to fight giant snake monsters but in truth, he hadn't signed up at all. Boone, like almost everyone else in his squad, had been drafted. This was his second tour though because Boone wanted his life to matter and keeping his buddies under Captain Keaton's command alive was the best way to do that as he saw things.

Collins was the unlucky bastard who drew the short straw and was out there on patrol around the edges of the village. Boone figured Damon was using Collins like a miner would use a canary in a coal mine. Collins was not only their early warning system but also added bait to help lure the creature they were after out of the jungle. Boone hated it but there wasn't a bloody thing he could do about it except keep his ears open and hope that if the monster did come after Collins that either he could make it into range of their cover fire or they could reach him in time, if Damon actually let them try.

As Boone worried about him, Collins crept through the jungle. Night had fallen quickly and the stars were obscured by thick clouds that blew in from the south. The air felt like rain. Collins cursed at the thought of it. Before shipping out to the Nam, he had loved the rain. Now, he fragging hated it. Getting soaked to the bone and listening to water sloshing around inside his combat boots was a special kind of hell unto itself and a hell he was sick of. Collins knew they were after a monster but not more than that. His grip on his M-14 grew tighter as Collins heard a twig snap to the right of his position. Collins ducked behind the trunk of a tree, keeping as still as he could, his ears sharp, trying to hear something that might tell him what he was up against.

Hushed voices were speaking in Vietnamese. Collins counted three distinct ones. That was his best guess based on what he could hear anyway. Odds were, there was a lot more than three Viet Cong closing in on him though. If there were three, there was likely an entire squad. No one had been expecting the N.V.A. to be here at the village. That creepy Damon guy sure hadn't indicated that they would be. His options royally sucked. Collins could stay where he was and hope the Viet Cong passed him by but if they did, they would catch his mates in the village utterly off-guard. But if he lit them up, Collins knew he was going to be on his own out here. He considered just making a run for the village but his gut told him that would be suicide.

Collins was carrying an M26 grenade. It had a kill radius of several meters and could inflict nasty wounds all the way out to around fifteen meters. Collins popped the M26's pin and lobbed it into the jungle towards where the voices were coming from. As it blew, Collins flung himself out from behind his cover and made a run for the village. The explosion of the fragmentation grenade lit up the night for the briefest of moments as Collins glanced back over his shoulder. He heard Viet

Cong troops screaming as shrapnel ripped into them. Collins' legs pumped beneath him, his breath coming in ragged gasps, as he pushed his body to its limits and beyond.

The surviving Viet Cong must have spotted him because a chorus of automatic fire from AK-47s roared. Muzzles flashed behind him from the depth of the jungle. Collins cleared the tree line and hit the ground rolling, trying to avoid being hit. He succeeded.

Damon and the others were already springing into action. The M 134 in the bed of the gun truck purred to life. Its barrels spun, hosing the trees, cutting through the trunks of the thinner trees and sending them toppling over. Green was screaming a battle cry, his hands tight on the M 134. Page was busy getting another belt ready for the minigun in case it was needed while Langley targeted the shadows of the jungle with his M-60. It chattered alongside the M 134.

Two Viet Cong came running out straight in the gun truck's line of fire. Bullets shredded their flesh and blew them apart in splatters of red.

The muzzle flashes in the jungle had stopped.

Damon shouted, "Cease fire!"

The M 134's barrels slowed, spinning to a stop. The night was silent again.

"Think we got 'em all?" Page whispered to Green.

"Shut up," Green snarled back at him.

Damon was watching the trees carefully. Something didn't feel right.

Then everything went to hell. . .

The snake came tearing through the trees, knocking them from its path as if they were nothing. Its head was the size of a fragging Jeep, fierce, blue eyes burning with rage and hunger. The width of its body was enormous. The thing had to be at least a couple of hundred feet long. The armor-like scales covering it gleamed in the pale light of the moon that leaked through the heavy clouds above. The thing was on a direct course for the gun truck, making a B line towards it.

"Frag!" Damon yelled, flinging himself out of the way as the giant snake darted past him. He hit the ground hard on his shoulder, a grunt escaping his lips. The snake was impossibly fast for something its size.

Green had opened up on the monster with the M 134. A stream of high velocity rounds sparked against the monster's scales. Some of them got penetration but most merely bounced off. Damon saw that the creature's scales appeared to be thicker on the crest of its head than other parts of its body. Langley was blasting the snake with his M-60 too. The barrels of Jager's UZIs spat bursts of fire at the giant snake as he ran out of its path. Bently didn't run though. He held his ground, his GAU-17's barrels spinning, taking his shot at the charging monster. All the firepower hitting the snake still did nothing to even slow the thing down, much less stop it.

The giant snake reached the gun truck. Its monstrous mouth opened. Giant jaws closed around the hood of the gun truck, shattering its engine block, as its front end was lifted up off the ground. Page was thrown from its rear, still clinging to a belt of ammo in his hands. Langley went rolling inside the gun truck's bed, slamming into its walls. Green managed to swing the M 134 around to bear on the giant snake, still pouring fire into the monster at point blank range. The rounds from the M 134 ripped a bloody swath across the top of the snake's head above its eyes. The snake picked the gun truck up entirely from the ground, swinging it about in the air, before smashing it back down. Bently didn't even have time to scream as the truck came down on top of him. His bones crunched inside of him, snapping into bits, as he was pulped beneath the truck's five tons of weight. Green was still clinging to the M 134 like a life line. His grip on it was all that kept him from being thrown out of the truck like Langley was. Langley's body bounced across the ground like a stone skipping on the surface of a lake. When it came to a stop, he was a mangled and broken mess with blood leaking from his mouth and one eye knocked loose from its socket dangling by a thin strand of sinew on the side of his face. He wouldn't be getting back up again.

Jager had vanished from Damon's field of view. The man had just disappeared. Damon took aim at the giant snake with his shotgun and squeezed the weapon's trigger. It thundered, blowing a huge hole in the snake's side. Bright red blood splashed out from the wound as the heavy slug tore into it. The snake slithered around to face him, its long body sliding over the squad's Jeep in the process. The Jeep was rolled over onto its side and pushed down into the dirt from the creature's weight. Damon stared into the snake's blue eyes which were close to the same size as he was as it emitted a shrill cry of anger at him. The only thing that saved him as the giant snake struck at him was Private Collins.

Private Collins reacted out of instinct more than anything else as he saw the snake getting ready to strike at Damon. He yanked another M26 grenade loose from his vest and hurled it into the creature's wide open mouth. The explosion sent blood flying as shrapnel shredded the softer, interior flesh of the snake. The monster's mouth snapped shut. The snake turned again, plunging away, back into the jungle.

Damon stood, frozen to the spot where he was standing, watching the snake disappear into the darkness of the night. It was a miracle they weren't all dead.

Collins jogged up to stand next to him.

Neither of them said a word to the other. Both of them were too stunned by the insanity of what had just happened to be able to speak.

****

Haley didn't know how his luck was crappy enough for him to end up on watch again tonight but it was. He took comfort in the fact that Berrong had ended up on it with him. The two of them sat in a foxhole along Firebase Seven's northern perimeter. There wasn't anyone left at the firebase who doubted that there was something seriously messed up out there in the jungle now. . . not after what had happened to Sergeants Red and Stevenson last night. Haley felt sick as an image of Sergeant Stevenson's melted face flashed through his mind. The new C.O., Captain Keaton, had doubled the number of people on watch. In addition to the posts like the foxhole he and Berrong were in, there were now pairs of soldiers walking the perimeter too.

Berrong was one of the few at the firebase who didn't smoke. Haley couldn't for the life of him understand how Berrong managed it. The stress they stayed under was so intense that Haley had become a pack a day guy if he could get his hands on enough smokes to do it.

"Take it easy, man," Berrong cautioned him as Haley discarded the cigarette he'd just finished only to light up another.

"Take it easy?" Haley glared at Berrong. "Really? We don't even know what's out there. It ain't just the Viet Cong anymore, buddy. Now we got a fragging monster to worry about too."

Berrong shrugged. "So what? I can promise you there's nothing out there a bullet or two won't kill. We just have to keep our eyes and ears open, man, make sure we see whatever's out there coming. That way we won't end up like those poor bastards the new C.O. buried today."

"Hey," Haley said. "Red was a good guy. I am going to miss that big, stupid lug."

Chuckling, Berrong grinned. "Yeah, miss him giving your arse latrine duty."

"Drop it," Haley warned, his voice cold and hard. He and Red had their differences but Haley had respected the sergeant.

"Sure," Berrong nodded. "It's hard to believe that there's more than the Viet Cong out there trying to kill us now."

"What? You don't believe in monsters?" Haley chuckled. "I didn't either until I saw that sergeant this morning. Nothing human could have done that."

"Whoa," Berrong stopped him. "I never said I didn't believe, man."

"Fragged up, ain't it?" Haley grunted.

"Yep," Berrong agreed.

"That thing just crept right up and killed them

both," Haley frowned.

"I'm keeping my eyes on the trees, Haley," Berrong said. "Maybe we should just shut up and focus on doing that together?"

"Heard a rumor that the new guys think the thing is some kind of snake," Haley commented.

Berrong looked to think over what he had just said.

"That's strange. The sergeants were murdered at night. Snakes are cold blooded. You wouldn't think they'd really be on the prowl after nightfall," Berrong pointed out. "And let's not forget the footprints in that foxhole. I've never seen a snake with feet, have you?"

"Yeah, I saw them too. I was right there with you, pal," Haley reminded him. "Guess we're not really gonna know what's out there until we see it ourselves."

Haley flinched as shots rang out from somewhere on the other side of the base.

The howitzer in the center of the base boomed, firing an illumination round. The flare it sent skyward, drifted back down towards the Earth, lighting up the night. In its glow, Haley and Berrong saw movement in the distant trees of the jungle. There were things moving around out there. Lots of them.

"Holy . . ." Haley muttered, tossing aside the cigarette he had been puffing on.

"What the hell?" Berrong rasped, leveling the

barrel of his M-14 at the shapes moving amid the trees. "If that's the Viet Cong, why aren't they shooting at us?"

The gunfire coming from the far side of the base intensified.

****

"Sit rep!" Captain Keaton yelled, rushing out of the T.O.C. Lieutenant Fogerty was close by as quick response squads rushed towards the perimeter of the camp.

"We don't really know yet, sir!" Lieutenant Fogerty shouted back at him, raising his voice so it could be heard over the gunfire that seemed to be coming from everywhere. "We've got contacts on all sides but none of them are returning fire or advancing on the base."

"Then what the hell are we wasting so much ammo for?" Captain Keaton snarled.

Lieutenant Forgerty's eyes bugged. He had no answer.

"Well don't just stand there, man, order a base wide cease fire!" Captain Keaton barked.

Darting into the Tactical Command Center, Lieutenant Fogerty rushed to do just that. His voice rang out of the speakers mounted on poles throughout Firebase Seven. "Cease fire unless fired upon! Cease fire!"

The sound of gunfire began to die down.

Captain Keaton snatched a pump action shotgun from the hands of a soldier standing near the entrance of the T.O.C. and ran for the firebase's perimeter. He wanted - needed - to see what was happening with his own eyes.

The howitzer in the center of the base spat more flares upwards into the sky. Two soldiers who were on watch and manning an M-60 aimed at the jungle were startled as Captain Keaton came running up to them.

"What did you see out there?" Captain Keaton yelled at them.

"Sir?" a private named Lorenzo stammered.

His buddy, another private by the name of Crow, said, "There were things out there in the trees, Captain. They weren't human."

Captain Keaton grabbed Private Crow by the front of his shirt. "Tell me about them!"

"Their eyes. . .their eyes were glowing out there," Private Crow blurted out. "They were glowing blue!"

"Captain Keaton!" Lieutenant Fogerty cried out, catching up to him. "Let him go!"

Releasing Private Crow, Captain Keaton spun around at Lieutenant Fogerty, punching him in the face. His fist smashed into Fogerty's jaw and sent the young officer reeling. Fogerty barely managed to regain his balance without toppling over. He looked at Captain Keaton in both shock and pain.

"Don't you dare tell me what to do, you little. .

." Captain Keaton raged. "I'm in command here now."

At that moment, something leaped through the air at Keaton. No one had seen the thing coming. It had blended perfectly into the shadows of the night, slithering along on its stomach until it had gotten into striking range. The creature was more snake than man though it was shaped like a human, having two arms and two legs. Its fangs gleamed in the light of the latest flare that had been shot up, eyes burning a bright blue. One of its clawed hands slashed through the air, raking across Captain Keaton's chest. He screamed in pain as they cut deep into his flesh, leaving bloody trails in their wake. Captain Keaton stumbled and collapsed but managed to sweep the barrel of his shotgun around towards the monster even as he fell. The shotgun thundered as he squeezed its trigger. The heavy slug it fired slammed into the monster, catching the thing in the dead center of its chest. The force of the blast picked the creature up from the ground where it had landed and flung it backwards. Even before its body had hit the ground, Privates Crow and Lorenzo were pouring fire into it with their M-14s. The creature's body twitched and jerked about as if it were having a seizure from the amount of rounds tearing into it. Bright red blood splattered outward with each round that entered its body.

"Frag me," Captain Keaton scrambled onto his

feet despite the pain from the wound the thing had dealt him. He worked the pump of his shotgun, chambering a fresh round.

More of the creatures were rushing out of the jungle now. . . racing towards the firebase. Private Crow dropped into position behind the M-60, bringing the machine gun to bear on them. Hot, spent casings were ejected from the big gun's side as its barrel blazed in a continuous series of flashes. One of the charging snake men took so many bullets to its chest that its rib cage seemed to explode. Another had its legs cut out from under it. Private Crow kept firing, trying to hold the snake creatures back but the things were just too fast. A couple of them made it through his field of fire despite the amount of rounds he was getting off.

Lieutenant Fogerty fired a burst from his M-14 into the stomach of the creature leaping at him. The bullets opened up the monster's guts. They spilled from its abdomen, swinging about wildly, flinging blood through the air. The burst didn't stop the creature though. It landed on Lieutenant Fogerty, knocking him to the ground. The young lieutenant screamed as the snake man plunged a clawed hand through his ribs. Bones broke, snapping, collapsing inward. Lieutenant Fogerty's eyes were wide as he watched the monster's hand come back out of his body clutching his still beating heart.

Private Lorenzo's rifle had a bayonet fixed to it. He stabbed the blade into the back of the snake man that had just torn out Lieutenant Fogerty's heart. The snake man gave an inhuman wail as Lorenzo twisted the blade of the bayonet between its shoulders. Private Lorenzo shoved forward, knocking the snake man over into mud, pinning it down there. The snake man kicked and thrashed about, straining to get loose. It was insanely strong. Even with the advantage of leverage and his entire body weight leaning into his keeping the monster down, Private Lorenzo knew the creature was about to overpower him. He squeezed his M-14's trigger in rapid succession, firing point blank into the monster above where his bayonet impaled it. The shots splattered the monster's bright red blood over his arms and onto his cheeks. The snake man stopped moving. Private Lorenzo ripped his bayonet free of its corpse and whirled about as another snake man took a swipe at his face, its claws flashing through the air in front of him, as he narrowly avoided its attack. His luck ended as the snake man he was engaged with sprang forward, its claws sinking into his shoulder, all the way to the bone. Private Lorenzo opened his mouth to scream but the snake man bit into his neck, silencing his cry.

Dripping blood from the gashes on his chest, Captain Keaton staggered towards the snake man. Its blue eyes locked onto him as he approached it and brought up the barrel of his pump action shotgun. The blast he fired pulped the snake man's chest, killing the monster instantly.

"They're falling back!" Private Crow shouted.

Captain Keaton looked around in disbelief. The snake creatures had them down to rights, the perimeter of the firebase breached, but now. . . they were retreating? It didn't make any sense. His gaze followed the last of the snake creatures that had attacked the watch position where he was. It really was running away and vanished back into the jungle from where it had come.

The cacophony of gunfire that been raging all around the perimeter of Firebase Seven fell silent.

"Thank God. It's over," Private Crow said, slumping against the sandbags his M-60 sat upon.

"For now," Captain Keaton said. "But you can dang well bet those things will be back."

****

The giant snake's attack had left them without a vehicle. It had overturned their Jeep, pressing it deep into the soft mud, and utterly wrecked the Devil's Horns, their gun truck. The thing had killed most of them too. Damon and Jager stood over Langley's broken and twisted corpse. . . or rather the bit of it that was sticking out underneath the mangled gun truck. Boone, Collins, Nicholson, and Green were the only survivors from the squad they had brought with them. And one couldn't really count Green. . . the man's mind had come apart at the seams. The private was in a catatonic state. They had tried everything they could to snap Green out of it but nothing worked. Jager, frustrated, had even stabbed him in the leg but still. . . Green just sat there staring off into nothingness.

Jager poked Bently's corpse with the toe of his boot. "Ain't no point in digging him out of there just to bury him again."

Damon turned his head to look over at Jager. "Where the hell did you go when the crap hit the fan anyway?"

"In case you didn't notice, my UZIs weren't hurting that thing at all, mate," Jager answered. "I was just trying to stay alive to fight again another day like everyone else."

Damon nodded slowly. He knew Jager wasn't a coward and had to admit, the man had a point. None of them had been prepared for the giant snake to hit them so hard and fast. It had come out of nowhere and caught them with their pants down, so to speak. Damon blamed himself for that. He had known what the creature likely was. . . he had just underestimated the thing. Damon promised himself that wouldn't happen again.

"Sir," Boone called to Damon. "Shouldn't we get moving? That thing could come back at any moment."

Jager cocked his head. "He's right. We're sitting ducks out here."

"I don't think it'll be back for a while," Damon said. "Collins fragged it up pretty bad."

"Thank you, sir," Collins grinned.

"That really was good work, Private," Damon assured him. "Likely we would all be dead if it wasn't for you."

"We all get lucky sometimes," Jager grunted.

"I really think we should get moving, sir," Boone pressed Damon.

Damon nodded. "Jager, you got point. We'll stick to the road and double time it back to Firebase Seven. With any luck, we can be there by the time the sun comes up."

Everyone fell in behind Jager as they all got moving. Nicholson got stuck with dragging along Green after they managed to get him onto his feet. Boone and Damon brought up the rear of the group together, walking side by side, watching the trees next to the sides of the road.

The squad marched in silence for nearly an hour before Boone got Damon's attention.

"Sir," Boone said.

"You don't have to call me that," Damon looked over at the private. Boone's hair was a short-cropped brown and his eyes green. He was slightly taller than average and fairly thin though well toned. Damon guessed he was somewhere in his early twenties. "My name is Damon."

Jager would have told him that he was getting soft as he aged but Damon didn't give a crap. Boone was one of those all American, young soldiers who seemed out of place in a war like the Nam. Damon couldn't help but feel bad for the kid.

"Are you and Jager really special ops?" Boone asked.

"Something like that, Private," Damon grunted. "Does it really matter?"

Boone shrugged as they kept walking. "I guess not."

"But that's not what you really wanted to ask me, was it?" Damon flashed a knowing smile.

"No, sir. . . uh, I mean. . .Damon," Boone answered.

"Go on then. Ask me whatever question you got burning you up inside," Damon urged him.

"Before we left the firebase. . ." Boone started and then paused as if choosing his next words carefully, "It wasn't a giant snake that killed Sergeant Stevenson and that guy they called Red. There were footprints in that foxhole. Ones that weren't made by anything human. Word got around quickly about that."

"You're pretty sharp for a private, Boone," Damon chuckled. "But if you think I know anything more than you do about what happened in that foxhole, you're wrong. That was something I wasn't expecting and am still processing myself."

"Really?" Boone's expression told Damon that

the kid didn't believe what he'd just said.

"Really," Damon assured Boone. "The intel I got before coming here suggested there was only one monster out here. That giant bastard that nearly killed us all back there in that village. . . that's what I was expecting to be hunting. The brass wants it dead . . .fast. If word about it got out and the folks at home blamed the thing on the chemicals we've been dumping in these jungles. . ."

"I get it," Boone nodded. "But then. . ."

"Yeah, now I'm stuck with a new problem too," Damon shook his head. "One I don't know crap about; as if the one I had wasn't big enough."

Boone grinned at Damon's choice of words.

Up ahead of them, Jager came to an abrupt halt. He held up a hand signaling for the rest of the squad to do the same. Damon left Boone to watch the rear and moved forward to join Jager.

"What's up?" Damon whispered.

Jager pointed up the road. "That's what's wrong. I think someone left us a message."

Damon squinted, peering through the darkness. There was still just enough light seeping through the gathering rain clouds for him to see what Jager had spotted. There were stakes driven into the dirt of the road. Each was as tall as a man with a rotting, slumping corpse dangling from it.

"Hold your positions," Damon ordered the rest of the squad. "If you see the crap hit the fan, then get the hell out of here."

Jager and Damon approached the corpses on the stakes. There were four of them in total that were spaced out across the entire width of the road. The corpses weren't bound to the stakes by ropes as Damon had assumed. Each of them had a jagged piece of what looked to be a human leg bone rammed through their chest into the wood of the stakes, impaling them and holding them in place. The corpses were all Viet Cong soldiers. One of them was headless, another's guts spilled out of him to coil at his feet. All of them were mutilated in some sickening manner.

"Now who do ya reckon did this?" Jager grunted.

"I think you already know my answer," Damon told him.

"I'm inclined to agree with it." Jager shifted the UZI he was holding from his right hand to his left and then reached out to grab the hair of one of the dead Viet Cong soldiers. He lifted the man's head to see the expression of terror his face was frozen in. The corpse's eyes were gone and their sockets hollow.

"Whatever they are, they sure made a mess of these poor bastards," Jager commented.

Damon motioned for the others to move up to their position. When they had, he said, "Things just went from bad to worse out here. We've got more company in the trees than we knew about.

Doesn't change anything though. Getting back to Firebase Seven as quickly as possible is still what we need to do."

"You heard the man," Jager snarled. "Onward."

Jager stayed on point, taking the lead, as they all got moving again.

****

Captain Keaton sat behind his desk in the tactical operations center of Firebase Seven staring at the man who had taken Lieutenant Fogerty's place as his second in command. Corporal Jack Reeves had a scar down his right cheek beneath the black hair that spilled out from underneath his helmet. There was drying blood, that wasn't his own, staining the front of his shirt. Reeves' expression was a hard one, cold and angry. Keaton's gut told him that Reeves had done a lot more time in the Nam than the young Lieutenant who was his predecessor had.

"You sent for me, sir," Corporal Reeves said.

"Yes I did, Corporal. Lieutenant Fogerty is dead," Captain Keaton frowned.

"A lot of good men are, sir," Corporal Reeves commented. "The last count puts us at seven dead with another four wounded."

Captain Keaton pushed back the chair he was sitting in and rose to his feet, walking around the desk to stand close to Corporal Reeves.

"Too many," he agreed. "So tell me, Corporal, how are we going to stop that from happening again?"

"The howitzers aren't going to help a fragging bit," Corporal Reeves spat. "These bastards we are up against. . . they're a hands on bunch, whatever the frag they are. We're going to need to better secure the perimeter of this firebase before the next time they hit us."

"I heard mines blowing last night," Captain Keaton said. "Do we have replacements on hand?"

"Only a handful, sir," Corporal Reeves answered. "Firebase Seven was never supposed to be here as long as it has been and our on hand stockpiles of ammo, etc. reflect that."

"But we're good on ammo for our rifles?" Captain Keaton watched the corporal closely, still appraising the man and his responses.

Corporal Reeves nodded. "Yes sir. At least on that front, we are good for the time being. Can't say the same for the M-60s. We're down to two of those and only a handful of belts for them after that Damon guy who flew in with you looted what we had."

"The M48. . . What kind of shape is it in?" Captain Keaton asked.

"She's good, sir," Corporal Reeves smiled. "A quick tune up and she's ready to roll."

"We don't need her to roll, Corporal. I just want her main gun ready when the crap hits the fan again," Captain Keaton ordered.

"I'll see that it is, sir. . . her fifty caliber too," Corporal Reeves assured him. "We got caught with our pants down last night, Captain. As you said, that's not going to happen again. Honestly I am surprised you didn't ask for Pratt as your second instead of me."

"I'll be needing Pratt in that tank, not out here running things with me," Captain Keaton said. "That's why you are here. I've read your service record. You've survived this war long enough to prove you can take orders and aren't a fragging, self-serving idiot."

"Thank you, sir," Corporal Reeves nodded. "I won't let you down."

"I know you won't," Captain Keaton scratched at the underside of his chin and the stubble growing there.

"If it's alright, sir, I'd like to get back out there now," Corporal Reeves told him.

"Go," Captain Keaton smiled, knowing for sure that he had picked the right man. "I want this base ready when night falls."

Corporal Reeves gave a sharp nod and exited the T.O.C. leaving Captain Keaton alone again. He sat back down in his chair and rubbed at his cheeks with the fingers of his right hand. As yet, there hadn't been any word from Damon and the squad the man had taken with him. Keaton didn't know if Damon had them running silent out there or if something had happened to them. Damon didn't care about a blasted thing except for carrying out his orders to destroy whatever monster the brass thought was out here. Only it hadn't turned out to be a monster lurking in the jungle after all, had it? No. It was a fragging, bloody army of monsters.

****

"I ain't touching that thing," Haley grumbled, staring down at the bullet ridden corpse on the ground.

The dead creature really was a snake man. There was no other way to describe it. The thing had scales instead of skin. It was completely naked except for the flies that swarmed it now in death. The scales were weird. They seemed to almost change colors depending on the angle you looked at them from – a mixture of black, yellow, green, and browns. The creature's arms were longer than a human's and reminded Haley of those of an ape. The thing's fingers ended in wickedly sharp, curved claws. Haley thanked God that this creature hadn't gotten the chance to use them. It had crept up on himself and Berrong during the attack on the base but the first illumination flare detonating in the night sky had saved them. The light from the flare had shocked the creature, causing it to hesitate, just enough to give them a chance to put a barrage of semi-automatic rifle rounds in it.

Berrong had a cloth held over his nose, trying to defend his nostrils against the stench that was coming from the corpse. "We gotta move it, Haley."

"It's not going to bite you," Chris laughed, walking up from behind where they were standing.

Berrong jumped at the sound of the medic's voice, swinging around to face him.

"Whoa," Chris exclaimed, raising up his hands in a gesture of surrender.

"What the frag are you doing out here, Chris?" Haley asked.

"Corporal Reeves sent me to check on you two and relieve you for a bit," Chris told them. "You guys are gonna be out here again on watch tonight, ya know? You need to get that thing buried and then grab some Zs while you still can."

"Come on, Haley," Berrong urged him. "Hurry up and get that thing into the hole we dug, man. Chris is right. I'm on the verge of falling asleep on my feet. We both need to log some hours in our bunks before . . ."

"Don't!" Haley stopped him. "Just don't say it. There's no reason to think that those things really are coming back tonight. Did you ever stop to think that we just might have scared the hell out of them? Last night could have been the first time they ever went up against hardcore, American troops. You saw how startled that thing was by the flare going up."

"I saw," Berrong admitted, "but I wouldn't get my hopes up if I were you. Those things were out for blood."

Chris moved by the two of them to squat down next to the snake man's corpse.

"What in the frag are you doing?" Haley stared at the medic.

"Checking something," Chris said.

Chris slipped gloves onto his hands. He reached out and shook the snake man as if making sure the creature was really dead. A swarm of flies took flight from the corpse.

"Be careful, Chris," Berrong warned.

"It's dead, Berrong," Chris assured him. "This isn't a horror film where the thing is suddenly going to leap up and kill me."

"Ha," Haley grunted. "You never know. It wasn't that long ago that any of us on this firebase would have believed you were out of your head if you told 'em there were things like that creature out there in the real world. Heck, I'm staring at the thing right now and I still have trouble believing it."

"Touché," Chris laughed. "But it ain't moving and appears to be rotting so. . ."

"Still pays to be cautious," Berrong urged.

"Anyway, what are you doing, man?" Haley pressed the medic.

Chris leaned over the snake man, poking the tips of his fingers between the thing's lips enough to pry its jaws open. Large fangs gleamed in the sunlight. Chris felt around inside the snake man's mouth. "Yep!" Chris declared. "Just like I suspected. This thing has some massive venom sacks in here. Toss me a knife, would you?"

Berrong unsheathed his and walked over to place it in Chris' hand.

"Thanks," Chris said. The medic worked, slicing away inside the snake man's mouth. A moment later, he held up the prize he had cut free. "You see this?"

"Venom gland, eh? Yeah, I see it," Haley quipped. "What about it?"

Chris was holding the venom gland with great care. "Well, I think the venom of these creatures is likely close to pure acid. If I am right, then it's proof that they are what killed Red and that new sergeant."

"I'd say we pretty much already know that," Berrong shook his head.

"Then call it just curiosity on my part," Chris shrugged. "I want to see just how powerful this stuff is."

Chris sat the venom gland down on the ground in front of him and very, very carefully cut it open. There was a hissing sound as the acid inside the gland touched the metal of the knife.

"Holy frag!" Berrong blurted out, his eyes bugging. "Is that stuff eating the metal?"

"Close enough to doing it," Chris nodded. "I've never heard of any living creature having this strong of venom. . . but it sure explains what happened to that sergeant. This snake man spat its venom on him and it melted away his skin and most of his facial bones, likely in seconds."

"All the more reason to make sure you shoot the fragging things before they get close to you," Haley said. "As if those claws they have wasn't reason enough. Frag, man."

"I really don't want to be here anymore," Berrong looked longingly at the closest of the firebase's two copter pads as if trying to will an extraction bird into materializing there.

"And how's that a new thing?" Haley mocked him. "None of us wanted to be here even before this crap, buddy."

"Haley's right," Chris said, standing up and handing Berrong his knife back. "We're stuck here and you know it. Those things being out there doesn't change anything with the brass and their plans. Now how about we get this thing buried, guys?"

Scowling, Haley grunted. He walked over and tried to pick up the snake man's corpse to drag it to the hole that had already been dug for it. "Frag! This thing is heavy! Somebody give me a hand."

Berrong didn't move. It was clear that he wasn't getting any closer to the snake man than he had to. Chris saw the fear that was still in Berrong's eyes and helped Haley himself. The two of them dragged the corpse to the hole and rolled it in. Haley was shoveling dirt onto the corpse when Berrong freaked out.

"We got movement in the trees!" Berrong shouted, leveling his M-14 at the jungle. He would have opened fire if it hadn't been for Chris. The medic moved quickly to snatch the rifle away from him.

"Hold up!" Chris yelled.

Haley looked at the forms emerging from the jungle. They weren't snake men or Viet Cong either. He breathed a sigh of relief, recognizing the men coming towards them. It was that Damon guy and some of the soldiers he had taken out with him.

****

Boone was fragging glad to be back at Firebase Seven. It was clear that the base had been attacked while they were gone but he didn't give a crap. Being back inside its perimeter was a hell of a lot better than being out in the jungle.

Damon dismissed the rest of the survivors, including his own man, Jager, but ordered Boone to stick with him as they went to pay Captain

Keaton a visit in the T.O.C.

Captain Keaton looked rough and utterly exhausted. His eyes were red and bloodshot. He glared at the two of them as they entered. Boone had seen the same sort of expression on Captain Keaton before and it always meant that hell was on its way.

"Thought you were dead," Captain Keaton grumbled without getting up to greet them. He sat behind his desk, scowling.

"You thought wrong," Damon said in a hard, cold voice.

"You wanna tell me where the rest of my men are, Damon?" Captain Keaton challenged the man in black. "Or where the gun truck you took out is?"

"Gone," Damon answered flatly. "Them and it. The creature I was sent to kill. . . It pains me to admit it but I underestimated the fragging thing. . . and worse, it isn't alone."

"No fragging kidding!" Captain Keaton raged. "We got our arses handed to us while you were gone, Damon!"

"Viet Cong?" Damon asked, taken aback by Captain Keaton's outburst.

"No. I don't know what the hell they were, Damon. The things weren't human. They were snakes on two legs," Captain Keaton caught his breath and shook his head. "Freaking monsters, Damon. That's what we had to fight off here."

Damon was silent for a few seconds. "That fits with what we ran into on the way back here."

"Does it now?" Captain Keaton snapped.

"It appears we've got more than one problem to attend to, Captain Keaton," Damon said. "Behaving as you are isn't going to solve anything. My orders prevented me from telling you anything more than I did before we left. And honestly, I didn't have a clue about these snake men as you call them either."

Boone watched as Captain Keaton struggled to calm down. "Captain, sir, the thing we ran into out there. . ."

"Ah yes. Damon's monster. You want to tell me exactly what it is?" Captain Keaton asked.

Damon grunted. "It's a snake. A really bloody big one. I'm talking at least a couple of hundred feet long with scales like armor."

"And it took out the gun truck?" Captain Keaton leaned forward.

Boone nodded. "And the Jeep. Those of us who survived had to walk back here, sir."

Damon slammed his hands, palms down, onto the top of Captain Keaton's desk. "The only thing that matters now is killing these creatures and making sure every last one of them is wiped out."

"Yeah," Captain Keaton chuckled darkly. "Good luck with that. God only knows how many of these snake men there are out there. There were dozens that hit us last night and I don't get the feeling that they were doing anything more than feeling us out, getting a sense of just how hard it would be to overrun us here."

"Look, Mr. Damon, I've known Captain Keaton for a long time. If he says there's an attack coming, you can count on it happening, sir," Boone spoke up. "Our best course may be to use this attack to hurt the bastards. We can use it as a chance to thin their numbers on our terms."

"That's excellent thinking," Damon smiled, impressed. "And then we can go after them come dawn and finish them off."

"Exactly," Boone nodded.

"That's a plan I can go along with," Captain Keaton agreed. "You're stuck here anyway, Damon. You'll be fighting for your life right next to the rest of us so you might as well join in defending this place."

"This firebase is unimportant," Damon commented, "but yes, I'll help with its defense."

Corporal Reeves came bursting into the T.O.C. All three of them turned to look at him as he skidded to a sudden halt upon seeing that Damon was present.

"Captain Keaton, sir," Corporal Reeves barked.

"What is it, Corporal?" Captain Keaton asked.

"I wanted to let you know that we've placed the last of the claymores we have on hand. Pratt also asked me to inform you that he and his crew are ready," Corporal Reeves reported.

"Thank you, Corporal," Captain Keaton nodded. "Is that all?"

"Yes sir," Corporal Reeves nodded.

"Pratt?" Damon asked. "He's the commander of the M48 Patton assigned to his base?"

"That's him," Captain Keaton confirmed.

"Come morning, I am going to be needing that tank," Damon said coldly.

"Come morning, if we're all still alive, it's yours," Captain Keaton agreed.

****

Pratt sat in *The Judge's* cupola, puffing on a cigarette. His crew was spread out around the M48 Patton. Jeff, the tank's loader, was leaning against her side armor, chewing on a mouthful of tobacco. He was as much of a redneck as the South could produce. Pete, the gunner, sat atop the armor plating covering *The Judge's* left treads. Anton, her driver, was pacing back and forth in front of *The Judge* with the same kind of nervous energy as he always seemed to have.

"Do you believe this fragging crap?" Jeff complained. "When did we go from being soldiers to being fragging monster slayers? We ain't Van Helsing, ya know?"

"Could be worse," Pete teased the grumpy loader.

"Oh, and how's that?" Jeff challenged him.

"These snake men things aren't going to be shooting any rockets at us," Pete said.

"Dang straight," Anton agreed. "And, thank God, we ain't infantry. Those poor bastards are going to get ripped up."

"Still ain't right," Jeff raged. "Things like those snake men shouldn't even exist in the real world."

"But they do," Pratt commented calmly.

Either Jeff hadn't heard him or didn't care what he had said because he kept going with his rant. "I mean, where the hell did they even come from? It's got to be all the Agent Orange and other crap the flyboys have been dropping in these jungles, right? That stuff is in the water, the air, everything out here."

"Since when did you become a scientist, buddy?" Anton shook his head.

"You got a better explanation?" Jeff glared at *The Judge's* dark-haired driver.

"I might," Pratt said, drawing all of their attention back to him where he sat in the cupola.

"I'd love to hear it, sir," Jeff said.

"Our former captain believed that there was a much simpler thing going on here. There are a lot of myths about snake beings in these parts. . . Naga, I think they call them. Most Naga are supposed to be good spirits. Well, that ain't the case with the one that lives here. The stories about it. . . they ain't nice, lads, not according to Whedon anyway. He thought maybe we invaders had done something to really tick off this local Naga and now it's out for everybody's blood."

"It?" Jeff stared up a Pratt. "I hate to remind you, sir, but there's a lot fragging more than just one of those snake men out there."

"Whedon was wrong about that, sure, but it doesn't mean he was wrong about the rest of it," Pratt sighed. "And frankly, all that matters is that when darkness falls this evening, it's going to be one hell of an interesting night. God knows that."

"Yeah, *The Judge'll* tear them a new one," Pete smirked.

"Amen to that!" Anton shouted.

"Crap," Pratt growled, as he glanced in the direction of the T.O.C. The man in black, Damon, had emerged from it and was walking their way. "Looks like we got company."

"Wonder what that bastard wants?" Jeff spat a mouthful of tobacco juice into the dirt.

"Guess we're about to find out," Pete sighed.

"Commander Pratt!" Damon called out, coming to a stop a few feet from *The Judge*.

"It's Damon, right? You don't have a rank I can call you by that I have heard about," Pratt greeted the man in black.

"Damon or Mr. Damon will serve," the man in black nodded.

"What can I help you with, Mr. Damon?"

Commander Pratt asked.

Damon looked over the M48 Patton. *The Judge* was almost thirty-one feet long and was nearly eleven feet high. Her main armament, a 90mm gun, was placed in the center of her turret. There was a .50 caliber mounted in the cupola that Commander Pratt was sitting in. Damon remembered from what he had read about M48 tanks that her max speed was around thirty miles per hour. *The Judge*'s armor looked tough as hell.

"Hey, man," Anton cackled at the man in black, "that's my lady you're checking out there."

"Anton," Commander Pratt snapped.

Damon took his eyes off *The Judge* to shoot an annoyed glare at Anton before returning his attention to Commander Pratt.

"Are your crew always so. . . dramatic?" Damon questioned him.

"I'm not big on the formalities and niceties, Mr. Damon," Commander Pratt said. "All I care about is that they do their jobs and do them fragging well."

Damon grunted in apparent approval. "I'd like a moment to discuss some things with you in private."

"Anything you have to say to me, you can say in front of my crew, Mr. Damon," Commander Pratt made no move to get down off the cupola. He stared down at the man in black, waiting on him to get on with it.

"There's more out there in this jungle than those snake men," Damon told them. "The squad I led out last night. . .we made contact with the target I was sent to eliminate."

"And you need my boys and *The Judge* to do that?" Commander Pratt frowned.

"Just what the hell is it you're after?" Pete asked.

Damon took a breath as if to steady himself before he spoke again, knowing the reaction he was about to get to what he said. "The target is a snake."

Pratt's crew all broke out in laughter, whooping and joking around before the commander reigned them in.

"A snake?" Commander Pratt stared at Damon in disbelief. "Seriously?"

"This snake is at least two hundred feet long with scales that are almost as tough as the armor on your tank," Damon answered. "It crushed a gun truck easily and wiped out over half of the men I took with me to the village where I had hoped to find it."

"Frag me," Jeff muttered.

Pete went pale and Anton just stood there with a shocked expression on his face.

"I assure you I am one hundred percent for real with this, Commander Pratt," Damon assured them all. "I watched the monster kill a good friend of my mine last night. This snake will not die easily. The howitzers of this base are useless against something like it. The creature moves far too quickly to ever be hit by their fire. Your tank however. . . I believe its main gun can get the job done."

"Assuming we all survive the attack tonight the new captain you brought with you is all fried up about . . .," Commander Pratt commented. "Then you can count on us, Mr. Damon. We'll go snake hunting with you."

****

Haley and Berrong had gotten some grub and rest. They were settled into the foxhole where they would be spending the night on watch. Berrong had somehow conned Corporal Reeves into letting them have one of the firebase's few remaining M-60s for their position. Haley was fragging glad to have the machine gun too. And it wasn't the only addition they had picked up for the night. Chris had returned to hang with them. The medic was armed with a pump action shotgun and had a determined look on his face.

"Hey, nice of you to join us, buddy," Berrong told him. "You know you didn't have to."

Chris shrugged. "I figured being out here was as good of a place as any to be. Besides, if you two get ripped up by those things out there, someone is going to have to stitch you up."

"Way to look on the bright side," Haley quipped. "Let's hope those things aren't able to get in that close again. I mean this time we'll be ready for the bastards."

Berrong patted the side of the M60 that sat on its tripod, aimed at the distant trees. "Frag yeah we're ready but hell man, if we're looking on the bright side and all, why not hope they don't come at all?"

"I'd say it's too late for that," Chris frowned as gunfire erupted from somewhere west of their foxhole.

Haley saw movement in the jungle. . . a lot of movement. Blue eyes glowed in the shadows among the trees.

"Here they come!" Berrong shouted.

The snake men burst out of the trees, sprinting towards the firebase. They came hissing, glowing blue eyes burning with primal rage. Berrong laid into them with the M60. Its heavy rounds tore into the creatures. One of the things screeched as a barrage of bullets opened up its chest in an explosion of bright red blood. Another crumpled to the dirt, its ruptured guts spilling from the wounds torn in its stomach. Still another was flung off-balance and sent reeling backwards as bullets cut a trail of gore from its crouch to the base of its neck. Berrong was sweeping the M60 about wildly, trying to hit as many of the creatures as he could. Haley aimed each of the bursts he fired from his M-14 much more carefully. He fired one that blew off the top of a snake man's head, sending bits of brain matter and bone fragments flying. Chris held his fire, his shotgun clutched tightly in his hands, ready for any of the creatures that made it through their field of fire. . . from the look of things, that was going to happen. There were more of the creatures than there had been during the previous attack.

Haley put a bullet through the center of a snake man's throat, silencing the thing's hissing battle cry. The snake men were so insanely fast that a few of them had already crossed the distance between the jungle and the firebase's perimeter. Haley swung around to engage one of the creatures that was only a few yards away from their foxhole. His M-14 chattered as a trio of rounds punched into the creature's chest. The snake man was sent tumbling backwards and fell over, dead, twitching in its death throes. Haley flinched as he heard Chris' shotgun thunder in the night next to him. The medic had targeted another snake man that was coming at them from the left. Chris' shot pulped the creature's groin. Shrieking, the snake man dropped onto its knees, hands covering the bloody mess between its legs. Haley finished it with a quick shot to the creature's forehead.

Berrong screamed as a snake man who had made it through his line of fire and come at him from the right flank jumped onto him. He rolled over, struggling against the monster as the thing's claws slashed at him. Blood flew as the flesh of the arm Berrong had swung up to protect himself with was shredded and cut to the bone. Haley came rushing to his defense. The snake man rose up, shrieking, as a burst from his M-14 hammered into its back. Berrong lashed out, kicking the snake man away from him and rolled out of the monster's reach. The firebase's central howitzer continued to pump illumination rounds into the sky but it was the distant sound of *The Judge*'s main gun firing that made Haley look up from Berrong's still desperate situation. When he did, Haley realized that with the M-60 no longer holding back the monsters pouring out from the jungle, their position was about to be overrun. He counted eight snake men that were almost upon them.

Out of nowhere, a thin, pale man in black came to their rescue. Haley thought his name was Jager or something German sounding anyway. The little guy came charging from behind them to meet the onrushing snake men, twin UZIs blazing in his hands. Snake men squealed and died as he cut a bloody swath through their ranks. By the time Jager's UZIs clicked empty, the ground was littered with their corpses and only three of the monsters were still standing. One of them was badly wounded, bright red blood leaking from bullet holes that spotted its upper body. Jager didn't try to reload his UZIs. The little man instead threw them away and slid two Ka-Bar 9140 knives out from where they were sheathed on his belt. Haley had never seen anyone so brave or stupid. The little guy was actually going to take on the snake men, alone, in hand-to-hand combat. The fastest of the snake men came at Jager, its claws streaking through the air towards his neck. Jager ducked the creature's swing, plunging a Ka-Bar blade into the monster's armpit. The snake man wailed in pain as Jager jerked the blade back out and sliced a long, nasty gash across its stomach with his other knife. The stunned creature stumbled backwards as Jager moved in for the kill, sinking the blades of both his Ka-Bars into the sides of its neck. The snake man collapsed as Jager again ripped the knives free. With a flick of his hand that was almost too fast for Haley to see, the little man threw one of his Ka-Bars at the other snake man rushing him. The knife spun end over end through the darkness, its blade gleaming in the light of the descending flares. The Ka-Bar smacked into the snake man's forehead, entering its skull so deeply that its tip emerged through the backside of the creature's head. All that remained of the wounded snake man as Jager took a look around to make sure that it was really the one only of the creatures left near him. Haley saved Jager the trouble of going after it, dispatching the monster with a series of cracking shots from his M-14. Jager sprinted back towards the foxhole where the others were.

While Haley had been distracted by Jager's battle with the approaching snake men, Berrong had continued to fight the one that he had been engaged with. Chris had jumped in, trying to keep the snake man off of him while Berrong scrambled to his feet. The medic wasn't an experienced fighter but had none the less come to his aid, slamming the butt of his shotgun into the snake man's stomach. The already wounded creature grunted and doubled over, blood still running from the holes Haley had blown in its back. The snake man had struck back by spraying the medic with its venom. Chris screamed as his skin burned and melted away where the venom landed on him. Flesh sloughed away from the bones of his hands and face. His eyes bubbled, liquifying inside their sockets. The skin of his fingers had already melted away, exposing the pointed tips of his finger bones as Chris raised his hands to cover what was left of his face.

Haley turned to see Chris' corpse flop over against the sandbags lining the foxhole. He could hear the sound of the young medic's flesh sizzling. The smell of it was horrible and made Haley gag. Only sheer willpower kept him from vomiting. Haley forced himself to look away, tasting the bile that had risen inside his throat. As he did so, Jager engaged the snake man that had killed Chris. The little killer leaped onto the snake man's back, taking the monster completely by surprise. Berrong had managed to recover enough to get his M-14 aimed at the snake man but was now forced to hold his fire as Jager wrestled with the creature. Jager forced the snake man's head back, reaching around to slash open the monster's throat.

The battle was still raging all around the firebase though their section of its perimeter was now clear. Jager cleaned the blades of his knives on his pants and re-sheathed the two Ka-Bars.

"Fragging bastard," Jager growled, spitting onto the snake man's still twitching body that had collapsed in front of him. He looked up at Berrong and Haley.

"You, stay here and hold the line if any more of those things show up," the little killer dressed in black barked at Haley. "You, you're with me! Come on!"

****

At the main entrance into Firebase Seven, the battle was far from over. Boone and Corporal Reeves were leading the soldiers there in the defense of the base against the dozens of monsters trying to overrun their position. The snake men had closed in and were now engaged in melee combat with many of the men around them. Boone blasted a snake man, bullets from his M-16 punching into the creature's side, as he saved the life of a private the monster had knocked to the ground and was about to slice open with its claws.

Corporal Reeves' shotgun thundered as its barrel flashed orange in the darkness of the night. The heavy round it fired plunged into and through the torso of a snake man, killing the monster instantly.

"We can't hold them!" Boone heard someone screaming in stark terror.

Frag that, Boone thought, they had to hold the monsters out or die trying. If they made it past them, the snake men would have full run of the firebase with nothing to stop the creatures from rampaging through it. Boone dodged the claws of a snake man that came charging at him and hammered the butt of his M-16 into the thing's gut. The snake man gave a pained grunt, hunching over, as Boone struck it again. He jerked the M-16 upwards and brought its butt down onto the monster's back, knocking the creature to the ground. The snake man rolled over, its mouth opening, but before the monster could spray him with its venom, Boone blew its head apart with a series of bursts from his M-16.

Corporal Reeves cried out as a wounded snake man he hadn't noticed lying on the ground near him reached up to sink its claws into his left thigh. The creature pulled him down and itself up at the same time as Corporal Reeves tried desperately to shove the monster off of him. His effort was in vain. There was no escaping the creature's grip with its claws imbedded in. The snake man hissed, hosing Corporal Reeves with venom. The monsters seemed to have learned that was the best way to fight back against the soldiers' guns and kill them quickly. A hit from their acid, even if it wasn't outright lethal, was enough to leave a man howling in pain and no longer able to fight as he burned. The stream of acid soaked Corporal Reeves' chest. His vest was burned into nothing almost instantly and the acid kept right on burning. Boone caught a glimpse of the white of Corporal Reeves' ribcage before he had to turn his attention to another snake man that was coming his way. The creature's face was twisted in a bizarre snarl as it hissed in fury at him. Boone was able to swing around his M-16 fast enough to get off a point blank burst into the monster before it closed the distance between them. The bullets slamming into the snake man knocked it off balance. The snake man stumbled backwards as Boone raised his M-16 up to brace its butt against his shoulder as he took aim at the creature. The weapon kicked against him as Boone took his shot. The snake man's head exploded like an overripe melon, bits of bone and brain matter flying amid splashing blood.

Boone hated to admit it but there appeared to be no choice but to fall back. There were just too many of the monsters and most of the soldiers who had been defending the firebase's entrance were dead, their bodies scattered and sprawled out all around him. Boone whirled about to make a run for it and found himself staring directly into the forward armor of *The Judge*. The twelve-ton tank came barreling towards him as Boone threw himself out of its path. Commander Pratt was in the tank's turret, blazing away at the onrushing snake men with the .50 caliber mounted there. The heavy machine gun cut a bloody swath through the ranks of the monsters. Screeching, hissing and squealing as bullets ripped them to shreds, the snake men's charge was finally ended. Those that weren't cut down by *The Judge*'s .50 caliber turned and ran back towards the cover of the jungle. The tank's sudden appearance had utterly changed the course of the battle. Boone whooped in triumph, cheering *The Judge* on as the tank rolled onward in pursuit of the fleeing snake men.

The Judge's main gun spoke. Its 90mm spat a round into the jungle that detonated in an explosion that sent bits of shattered trees flying like shrapnel. Some of the trees that were left standing near where the round hit had been set ablaze by the blast.

Commander Pratt slapped the tank's armor. "Halt! This is fragging far enough, Anton! Back us up!"

The tank lurched to a stop and then slowly backed up, returning to being inside the firebase's perimeter. The soldiers left alive in the immediate area rallied around it except for Boone. He could see that with the Patton holding the line, this section of Firebase Seven was as secure as it was going to be and a hell of a lot better off than the places where scattered gunfire still sounded in the night.

****

Captain Keaton had joined up with the squad on the firebase's eastern side where the snake men were threatening to break through. By time he got there, only three of the original squad assigned to the position were alive and one of them was badly wounded, sprawled out on the ground trying to stuff his intestines back inside of himself. The man's skin was pale and his eyes wide with shock as he scooped up handfuls of his own entrails, thick, red slicked purple chords, and cramped them through the wound a snake man's claws had torn across his stomach. The wounded man's head snapped backwards atop his shoulders as a bullet pierced his skull. Damon had fired the shot from the 1911 in his right hand.

"He was dead and you know it," Damon shouted at him, snapping Captain Keaton out of his shock. "Now get your fragging head back in the ballgame, Captain!"

That wasn't a problem for Captain Keaton.

The snake man that tackled him left him no choice but to do so. The thing plowed into him, knocking the captain from his feet. Captain Keaton slammed an elbow into the snake man's jaw as the thing hissed and spat out a mouthful of venom. The blow turned the monster's head enough so that the venom struck the dirt next to where the two of them wrestled instead of burning off his face. Grunting, Captain Keaton was able to roll, bringing the snake man along with him. The move left the creature struggling under him, the monster's advantage taken away from it. Captain Keaton knew he had to move fast. There was no time for him to draw the pistol holstered on his hip and he had lost his hold on his rifle when the thing had taken him down. Captain Keaton smashed his forehead into the monster's, stunning the snake man, and allowing him to leap away from it. He put just enough space between himself and the creature for him to be able to draw his sidearm. The captain's pistol cracked in rapid succession as he fired several rounds that tore into the snake man and sent bright red blood splattering.

Captain Keaton stumbled onto his feet as another snake man charged him. He swung up his pistol but the snake man was stopped before he could get off a shot. Boone came running up from behind the creature, spearing the thing with a bayonet affixed to the barrel of the M-16 he carried. The snake man shrieked as the bayonet pierced its scales. Captain Keaton watched Boone give the blade a hard twist inside the monster's body before wrenching the bayonet free. The snake man toppled to the ground, its face twisted in a grimace of pain. Boone kicked the creature in the face as it tried to get up, driving it back down, and then fired a point blank burst into the snake man to make sure it wasn't going to try again.

"What the hell?" Captain Keaton asked, looking beyond Boone to see the snake men suddenly disengaging with the remaining men under his command and sprinting away into the shadows of the night. It made no sense. The fragging things had them dead to rights. If they had just pressed on with their attack there would have been no stopping them.

Boone looked as shocked as he was. That didn't stop Boone from taking a shot at the fleeing snake men though. His M-16 barked, sending one of the monsters back to whatever hell it had crawled out of before the creature could reach the cover of the trees.

"The main entrance is secure, sir!" Boone yelled.

Captain Keaton listened to the night around them. The sounds of gunfire, hissing, and screaming had all stopped. The battle was over as quickly as it had begun. Captain Keaton didn't have any idea why but he wasn't going to look a gift horse in the mouth.

"Stay here with those two," Captain Keaton pointed at the only other surviving soldiers. "Be ready to hold this ground if those things decide to change their minds."

"Yes sir," Boone nodded.

Damon had already left. Captain Keaton had seen the man in black racing off in the direction of the tactical command center. He ran after Damon, legs pumping under him as fast as they could. Captain Keaton caught up to Damon as the man in black came to a stop at the entrance to the T.O.C.

"Wanna tell me what in the hell you're doing?" Captain Keaton raged.

"The snake men have fallen back all along the base's perimeter," Damon answered. "Don't you see what that means?"

Captain Keaton stared at Damon. He had no clue what the man in black was talking about.

"The Naga itself has to be coming!" Damon snapped.

"The . . . what?" Captain Keaton stammered.

"We need to get the men withdrawn into the center of the base as quickly as possible. I've seen what that thing can do, Captain. Our only hope is gathering everyone together to make a stand as a unified front," Damon hurriedly explained.

****

There were cries going up all over the

firebase, voices shouting that everyone needed to withdraw and regroup in its center. Haley heard them and wondered just what the hell was going on. He could see that Jager was wondering the same thing. Something was up. . .something fragging bad. It didn't make any sense because the snake men were withdrawing everywhere that he and Jager showed up as they made their way around the base's perimeter in an attempt to offer support to those who needed it. No one did. The entire perimeter seemed to be littered with the corpses of snake men and soldiers who had died defending it. The soldiers who had survived the snake men's onslaught were obeying the shouted order being passed around and falling back.

Haley and Jager were met by Berrong as they raced towards the center of Firebase Seven. Berrong's wounded arm was bound with cloth torn from his shirt as he cradled it to his chest. He clutched a pistol in his good hand and appeared very much to still be in the fight. Haley was just glad to see that his friend was okay. Berrong joined up with them.

"There!" Jager pointed up ahead of them. There was a bunch of soldiers who were heaving around sandbags and building a makeshift barricade in the center of the base. Haley saw that Captain Keaton and Jager's C.O., Damon, were among them.

"Jager!" Damon shouted as he saw them

coming. "Get the frag over here!"

The little killer increased his pace and leaped over the bags that were already in place, racing towards where Damon was

Haley spotted Anderson. He was the chief artillery officer of the firebase. Things really did have to be bad if Anderson was out here with everyone else hauling sandbags.

"Hey," Haley said, running up to join Anderson in his work. "What's going on?"

"Captain Keaton ordered it," Anderson huffed. "He thinks those things out there pulled back because something worse is on its way here."

Haley slammed the sandbag he was moving into place on the wall that was being built and then stopped to stare at Anderson.

"Something worse?" Haley asked. "What the frag could be worse than an army of snake men who spit acid venom?"

"I'll tell you that, Private," Jager said, having returned from speaking with his C.O. "I've seen it."

"Seen what?" Haley croaked. Jager didn't seem like the sort of man who was afraid of anything but right now. . . there had been a half-hidden edge of fear in his voice.

"The Naga. . ." Jager answered. "At least that's what your previous captain here called it."

Berrong was nodding. "I heard about that. Most of us did. We all thought Whedon was a bit crazy despite all the weirdness that was going on."

Jager glanced at Berrong. "You should get that arm seen to, Private."

"It can wait, sir," Berrong grunted.

"Huh. It'll likely have to," Jager nodded. "If the Naga is coming, it'll be here soon. That thing is fast. . . faster than it has any fragging right to be."

"Copy that, man, but . . ." Haley pressed the little killer in black.

"It's a snake," Jager told them. "A fragging big snake. . .scales like armor and a hellish rage. The thing took out a gun truck and nearly killed the entire squad that accompanied us hired guns out to that village. One of Keaton's boys, Collins, he managed to hurt the thing enough to drive it off or we'd all be dead."

"Dang right I did," Collins said, walking up to them. "Grenade straight into its mouth."

"Collins!" Jager exclaimed, turning to slap him on the shoulder. "I thought you were dead."

"No, sir," Collins grinned. "Just ended up on the far side of the battle tonight."

"Don't call me sir," Jager snarled.

Haley looked around and it began to sink in just how many had died in the snake men's attack. If everyone left was here in the center of the firebase, there were only around two dozen survivors in total. The creatures had hurt them. . . bad.

"Wait. . ." Haley butted in. "Where's *The Judge*?"

****

The Judge sat on the main road that led into the firebase. Commander Pratt was still in its cupola, his palms sweaty where they clutched the .50 caliber mounted there. The night was muggy but the interior of the tank below him felt like it was hotter than hell. Heat from the engine and the main gun bled into it. Anton had it the worst in the driver's seat, strapped in, and sweating like a pig. Jeff and Pete were sweating too.

"Don't know what the idiot Damon wants us out here for," Pete complained.

"Yeah," Jeff agreed. "Those snake things are gone, guys. I'm pretty sure they ain't coming back either."

"At least not tonight. . ." Anton snorted. "We handed them their arses pretty good."

"Did we?" Pete asked. "I'm not so sure about that."

Commander Pratt remained silent, only halfway listening to them. His eyes were on the distant trees and the shadows of the jungle. He knew why Damon had ordered them to take up position here. Normally, Commander Pratt would never have kept anything from the others but this time was different. He figured even with seeing things like the snake men with their own eyes they wouldn't believe what they were about to be up against or they would freak out and lose their crap. Commander Pratt couldn't afford that right now. He needed them all at their best and since they were taking things in their stride, thinking it was them who had driven away the snake men, there didn't seem to be a reason to share what he knew.

The monster out there that was coming for them was like something out of a nightmare according to Damon. He believed the C.I.A. man too. Spooks like Damon didn't scare easily but Commander Pratt could tell just how worried he was about any of them making it through the night. Damon believed *The Judge* was their best shot at stopping the giant snake that was on its way to the firebase. He was counting on the tank's main gun being able to penetrate the snake's armor-like scales and frag the thing up enough to take it out. Commander Pratt hoped Damon was right. Odds were *The Judge* would only get off one shot, maybe two, before the thing took her out of action.

"Hey, boss," Pete called to him, tearing Commander Pratt's focus away from the trees and his mind out of the dark thoughts it had been lost in. "I got movement out there at eleven o'clock."

Commander Pratt stood up straighter, his eyes straining to see whatever *The Judge's* gunner had just told him about.

"You want me to light up the contact, sir?"

Pete asked, maybe a tad too much trigger happiness in his voice.

"Hold your fire," Commander Pratt ordered. "We need to make sure of our target."

"Yes sir," Pete barked.

Commander Pratt was still staring into the trees but even so, he heard the monster approaching before he saw it. Trees were being snapped in two, flung aside, out of the thing's path, broken by its strength, cracking against the armor-like scales that covered the enormous snake's body. He gawked in awe and terror at the gigantic monster as it came into view. The snake had to be hundreds of feet long. A forked tongue, as long as a grown man, flicked in and out the barely open slit of its mouth, tasting the air. The colors of the snake's scales seemed to change before his very eyes. They were black, green, yellow, brown, dull orange . . . all changing, mingling, causing the monster to blend into its surroundings. Pratt swallowed hard as his heart pounded rapidly against his ribs. He'd seen a lot of death and action over the years but this snake. . . it was an abomination. The huge snake was like a demon straight out of the depths of hell itself. A thing like it had no right existing on the Earth.

"I have that thing in my sights, sir!" Pete yelled from below him. There was shock equal to what he was feeling in the gunner's voice.

"Take your shot!" Commander Pratt ordered

as he opened up on the monster himself with *The Judge*'s .50 caliber.

The entire tank rocked backwards from the recoil of its main gun as Pete fired it. The 90mm was designed to take out other armored units, bunkers, and aircraft. The high velocity round exploded out the gun's barrel, speeding towards the gigantic snake. It punched through the scales covering the giant snake's side as the beast twisted about in an attempt to dodge the round. Blood exploded outward from the hole where the shot had entered as the round detonated inside the giant snake. The creature rose up, several dozen feet of its hulking body rising from the ground, as its blazing blue eyes locked onto *The Judge,* burning with primal fury.

"You're good to go!" Commander Pratt heard Jeff yelling at Pete. That meant another 90mm round was locked and loaded.

The Judge's .50 caliber continued to roar as Commander Pratt hosed the giant snake with a continuous stream of fire. Orange tracer rounds streaked through the night. The rounds from the .50 caliber were getting penetration despite the snake's tough scales. Commander Pratt could see that he was royally ticking off the monster too as he raised the .50 caliber's barrel upwards, cutting along the snake's exposed underside where it had risen up from the ground.

Inside *The Judge*, Anton and Pete were

struggling to bring the main gun to bear on the snake again. As big as it was, the thing was still just too dang fast. The tank rolled backwards trying to get in line for another shot. . . but then the giant snake finally struck back.

The snake struck at *The Judge*. Its massive head came at the tank in a blinding flash. Commander Pratt was knocked from the tank's cupola and sent rolling across the ground. He grunted in pain, his shoulder dislocating from the impact. Commander Pratt clutched at his messed-up shoulder with his good hand, stumbling up onto his feet. The snake had kept its mouth closed. Its intent had never been to bite *The Judge* as he had thought it was trying to do. No, the thing was smarter than that. The snake had kept its mouth closed to protect itself from the fire of the tank's .50 caliber. It had just wanted a hold on *The Judge*. Commander Pratt had trouble believing what he was seeing and almost wondered if he had hit his head too.

The Judge had been rolling slowly backwards as the snake made its grab for it. The giant snake nudged the twelve-ton tank up with the tip of its head so that it could sling around and under to coil about it. *The Judge's* armor creaked and groaned from the pressure that was being applied to it by the snake. The thing was winding tighter and tighter about *The Judge,* trying to crush it. Anton, Pete, and Jeff were knocked around inside the tank. Jeff had scrambled up, trying to close its top hatch. The .50 caliber had already been ripped away from the cupola and the main gun bent sideways by the snake's attack.

"We're gonna die, man!" Jeff yelled, finally getting the hatch slammed closed.

"Brace yourselves!" Pete shouted before his face was flung into the gunner's scope. His teeth crunched against its metal. He spat out shattered pieces of them in a wad of blood. Red leaked down over his chin.

Anton cried out as the front of the tank began to cave in towards him where he sat in the driver's seat. Jeff bounced from one side of *The Judge's* interior to the other. Instruments were smashed as he crashed into them and they ripped at his body.

Commander Pratt stared in awe and horror as the snake lifted the *Judge* from where it had entwined her and took her a good twenty feet up into the air. Then the giant snake released the tank, flinging it away as its body uncoiled. *The Judge* struck the ground with a massive thud, rolling and bouncing, like a toy tossed away by an angry child.

A good portion of *The Judge's* armor was bent and warped. When the tank came to a stop, it lay on its side, smoking. Its main gun had been snapped in half. Commander Pratt could see that the tank was done for. He wanted to run to it, try to help anyone left alive inside the heavy vehicle to get out of it, but never got the chance. The giant snake was barreling towards him. Commander Pratt didn't really think it was coming after *him* so much as it was just heading onward into the firebase. He turned to run as the snake slithered over him, crushing him into the earth. The last thing Commander Pratt heard were the sounds of his own bones breaking and snapping beneath the monster's body.

****

"Here it comes!" Captain Keaton barked from where he stood in the center of the firing line the remaining soldiers of Firebase Seven had set up. "Light it up!"

Haley was mumbling a prayer as Jager's UZIs started roaring beside him. Berrong's pistol was cracking in rapid succession as he emptied its magazine at the approaching snake. The monster tore through the tactical command center as if it were paper on its way towards them, crushing it into rubble.

Boone stood next to Captain Keaton as their M-16s chattered away on full auto. Damon hoisted an L.A.W. up, getting it ready to fire. Collins and Green were pouring rounds into the giant snake too.

Nicholson worked the pump of his shotgun between each shot he took, chambering fresh rounds, one after another. Everyone was focusing their fire on the giant snake. Sparks flew where shots that lacked the power to pierce its scales bounced harmlessly away.

Captain Keaton couldn't believe the monster was taking it all and still coming but it was. The giant snake crashed into and through the piled-up sandbags the firing line was using for cover. Men screamed as the monster's body slithered over them, grinding them into the ground beneath its weight. Damon was cursing like a sailor. The snake had closed on them too quickly for him to get a bead on it with the L.A.W. He clutched the L.A.W. tight, throwing himself out of the snake's path. A few others escaped the monster too, running for their lives. Haley was one of them. He looked back to see Berrong die. Blood squirted out from under the snake's massive body where he had been dragged down beneath it. Then the snake was through their position. It kept going, deeper into the base, but Haley knew that was just so that the thing could swing itself around to come at those who had survived again.

Boone saw Jager actually take off running after the snake. The little man had discarded his spent UZIs and had his Ka-Bars out in his hands. Nicholson ran after him. The two of them had to be fragging crazy. Nicholson was cramming rounds into his shotgun as he ran, having already emptied its initial load into the snake.

"Fall back!" Captain Keaton was yelling but no one had any idea where in the hell they were supposed to fall back to. There was nowhere safe from the giant monster they were engaged with.

The snake's tail flicked about just as Jager reached it. The little killer never got to use his knives. The tail slammed into him, the impact lifting his body from the ground and flinging it through the air to land several yards away from where he had been. His chest was caved inward and blood poured from his open mouth into the dirt. Nicholson skidded to a halt just short of the snake's flicking tail and fired his shotgun. The weapon boomed. The heavy slug it spat out blew a chunk of red slicked scales from the snake's tail.

Having made its turn, the snake came around at the survivors. It scooped Nicholson up in its mouth before the poor bastard even had time to scream, swallowing him whole.

Damon got his shot at the monster. The L.A.W. launched its 66mm rocket in a burst of smoke and flame. The rocket flew straight and true at where Damon had been aiming for. It hit the giant snake's head, exploding there. The giant snake lurched to a stop, its head swaying about twelve feet or more above the ground, clearly stunned by the blast. The hole that the rocket had torn in it was a bad one. Brain matter oozed out from the wound blown in its skull. Damon had really hurt the monster . . .but not enough to kill it yet.

"Hit it with everything you've got, boys!" Captain Keaton yelled, trying to rally those who were still alive around him. . . and they did. A fresh cacophony of gunfire erupted in the firebase. Captain Keaton could see that it wasn't going to be enough to stop the monster. Out of the corner of his eye, Captain Keaton spotted a high explosive round for one of the base's howitzers sitting next to one of the large canons. He ran to retrieve it as the giant snake came rushing forward.

Haley was unable to escape the snake this time. Its mouth closed on him, snapping his spine in two, as the snake yanked him into the air. His legs and arms dangled wildly about in the air as the snake shook its head in furious anger at the pain it had to be in from the wounds it had taken.

Damon saw that Boone, Collins, and Green were the only others left alive other than Keaton as the giant snake thrashed about killing everyone else with the blinding speed of the apex predator that it was.

"Hey!" Captain Keaton shouted at the snake. "I've got something for you, you bastard!"

The giant snake's head whipped around, its blue eyes catching Captain Keaton in their sight. The captain remained perfectly still holding onto a H.E. shell as the snake sprang at him, its mouth opening wide. The snake swept Captain Keaton up in its mouth. Half a second later, the H.E.

round blew. The giant snake's head burst apart in an explosion of gray brain matter, bright red blood, and white shards of skull and jaw bones. Its headless body thudded onto the ground but continued to roll and twist about in its death throes. Damon and the others scattered, getting the hell away from the monster. Even though it was dead. . . the thing was still dangerous as hell until its body stopped moving.

****

Firebase Seven was in utter ruins. Most of its structures were broken and crushed. There were corpses lying about in every direction as Boone looked around. The sun was rising and soon those bodies were going to start to really stink.

Damon was standing near the headless corpse of the giant snake, taking photos of it. Boone walked up to him. Though Damon wasn't actually in Boone's chain of command, not exactly, he was more than willing to defer to him as his own C.O.'s orders had been to lend support to the C.I.A. operative.

"What's all that about?" Boone asked, gesturing at the camera in Damon's hands.

"Evidence. . .proof. . .We can't carry this thing out of here with us, ya know," Damon shrugged.

"Do you really think anyone will believe you even with whatever photos you take?" Boone frowned.

"My superiors will," Damon assured him. "The rest of the world. . . they'll never hear a word about what happened here. Count on that."

"But all the people who died. . ." Boone waved a hand in the direction of the closest corpses.

"Killed by enemy action," Damon grunted. "This base was overrun by the Viet Cong. They died fighting bravely for their country and each other."

"Copy that," Boone nodded, knowing he no other choice. He figured that if he contradicted whatever lies Damon and his superiors told when they got back home, they would shut him up quickly, no matter what it took to do it.

The firebase's communications had been knocked out in the battle with the giant snake. Their only option was to head out on foot for the next closest American base. Collins, Green, and Commander Pratt were busy rounding up ammo and supplies for that long march. No one had even known the commander was alive until an hour after the battle with the giant snake was over. He had come walking up to them where they had gathered at what was left of Firebase Seven's mess. All of them were sad to hear that *The Judge* and the rest of her crew had been lost too. The snake had destroyed the M48 Patton tank on its way to engage them. Commander Pratt had confirmed the deaths of his crew inside the crumpled mass of metal that had once been *The Judge*. The loss of his people had taken a dire toll on the commander. No longer was Pratt a man who exuded confidence and strength. He was nothing more than a pale shadow of who he used to be, haggard, and jumpy.

Damon snapped a final picture of the giant snake and then shrugged of the backpack he was wearing to slip the small Nikon into it. "You ready?" he asked.

"As I am going to be," Boone answered honestly. He was very much ready to be gone from Firebase Seven but Boone also knew what was likely waiting for them out in the jungle.

Boone and Damon walked together to where the others were finishing up. Green was loaded down with gear as was Collins. Their backpacks bulged from all the things that were shoved into them. Commander Pratt wasn't carrying anything but a pistol holstered on one hip and a canteen hanging from his belt.

"Guess it's time, huh?" Commander Pratt asked wearily.

"Daylight's wasting," Boone nodded, giving Green and Collins a disapproving glare. "Think you guys got enough crap in those packs?"

"Wanted to be prepared, sir," Green answered.

Boone grunted. Making them dump some of it wasn't worth the time it would cost. With a heavy sigh, Boone looked over at Damon. "I'll take point then."

The small group left the wreckage of Firebase Seven behind, heading south. The day was hot and the blazing sun did nothing to help matters. Boone almost wished it would rain. . . almost . . . though that would bring an entirely new set of problems with it. His best estimate put the closest U.S. Base several days walk away. Boone pressed everyone hard, wanting to get as much ground covered before the sun went down as possible. Once it did, there was a good chance that they would have company. The snake men hadn't returned to attack the firebase again after the giant snake had been slain but that didn't mean the things were done with them. The death of the creature they likely worshipped as their god might have driven them off but if their fear turned to anger. . . well, Boone didn't want to think about that.

The remainder of the day passed uneventfully. They paused for a meal of MREs late in the afternoon and quickly got moving again. Boone stayed on point, leading the others through the jungle. Damon brought up the rear, keeping a watchful eye out for any of the snake men that might be tailing them.

Something didn't feel right to Boone but he couldn't put his finger on what it was. He considered bringing the group to a halt but thought better of it. Such a move would only tip off the snake men that they knew the creatures were out there, watching them, if he made it. Neither he nor anyone else among them saw the attack coming.

AK-47 fire erupted from all around them. Green died as bullets punched through his chest and lungs. Boone and Collins threw themselves flat, managing not to be hit. Damon wasn't so lucky even though he did the same. A round entered the right side of his body, plunging deep into the C.I.A. operative's guts. Commander Pratt took a bullet to the head, killing him instantly.

Boone returned fire, spraying bullets into the trees, trying to drive their attackers back. Collins yanked a grenade from his belt, pulling its pin. He lobbed it in the direction the bulk of the enemy fire was coming from. The AK-47s there fell silent in the wake of its explosion.

"Got the bastards!" Collins laughed with a deranged grin parting his lips.

Damon, though wounded, was very much still in the fight. He swung up his M-16, targeting a Viet Cong soldier that came out of the trees, charging at him with a bayonet affixed to the barrel of his rifle. Damon squeezed the trigger of his weapon, firing into the soldier at near point blank range. The Viet Cong was flung backwards as Damon's well aimed burst made a mess of his face.

Collins leaped to his feet as more of the Viet Cong emerged from the trees. He cut another one of the enemy soldiers down before his body was riddled with bullets. Boone watched Collins fall and knew that he was dead. Only he and Damon were left alive and they were massively outnumbered. Boone counted more than a dozen Viet Cong coming at them. His M-16 roared as he hosed two of them with a burst of rounds that sent the bastards to hell.

Boone heard Damon cry out. His head jerked around in the C.I.A. operative's direction and he saw that one of the Viet Cong had closed in on Damon. The Viet Cong was snarling, the bayonet mounted on the barrel of his AK-47 sunk deep into Damon's chest. Damon had lost his rifle and was struggling to keep the soldier from driving the blade of the bayonet any deeper. Another Viet Cong rushed up beside the first, pistol in hand. It cracked as he fired a shot, point blank, into Damon's forehead.

Pain surged through Boone's back. He looked down and saw a trio of exit wounds in his chest. His eyes wide, blood rising inside his throat, Boone's rifle fell from his hands. The world spun around him as he tried to stay on his feet. His hand reached for the pistol holstered on his belt but never made it there. More bullets hammered into his body, twisting him about. Boone toppled over, face first, onto the ground. A puddle of red seeped out from his wounds around him where he lay. . . and then, his pain stopped along with the beating of his heart.

EPILOGUE

Agent Forrester looked up from the mountain of paperwork on his desk as Reid's knuckles rapped against the side of the open door of his office.

"Still no word?" Agent Forrester asked, seeing Reid's expression.

"None at all," Reid answered. "I think we're going to have to assume that Damon and his people are K.I.A. On the bright side though, sir, we haven't received any more accounts of villages being wiped out in the area Firebase Seven was located in. The entire region there seems to have returned to normal. . . well, as normal as it can in the middle of a war. The Viet Cong have reclaimed the area and so far are managing to hold it."

"Are you suggesting that we just close this matter, Agent Reid, and be done with the whole thing?" Agent Forrester frowned.

"I am, sir," Reid nodded. "If there was some kind of mutated creature there, Damon's team must have eliminated it."

"Fine," Agent Forrester conceded. "Make it all disappear then."

"Yes sir," Reid flashed him a smile and left his office.

THE END

AUTHOR BIO

Eric S Brown is the author of numerous book series including the Bigfoot War series, the Psi-Mechs Inc. series, the Kaiju Apocalypse series (with Jason Cordova), the Crypto-Squad series (with Jason Brannon), the Homeworld series (With Tony Faville and Jason Cordova), the Jack Bunny Bam series, and the A Pack of Wolves series. Some of his stand alone books include War of the Worlds plus Blood Guts and Zombies, Casper Alamo (with Jason Brannon), Sasquatch Island, Day of the Sasquatch, Bigfoot, Crashed, World War of the Dead, Last Stand in a Dead Land, Sasquatch Lake, Kaiju Armageddon, Megalodon, Megalodon Apocalypse, Kraken, Alien Battalion, The Last Fleet, and From the Snow They Came to name only a few. His short fiction has been published hundreds of times in the small press in beyond including markets like the Onward Drake and Black Tide Rising anthologies from Baen Books, the Grantville Gazette, the SNAFU Military horror anthology series, and Walmart World magazine. He has done the novelizations for such films as Boggy Creek: The Legend is True (Studio 3 Entertainment) and The Bloody Rage of Bigfoot (Great Lake films). The first book of his Bigfoot War series was adapted into a feature film by Origin Releasing in 2014. Werewolf Massacre at Hell's Gate was the second of his books to be adapted into film in 2015. Major Japanese publisher, Takeshobo, bought the reprint rights to his Kaiju Apocalypse series (with Jason Cordova) and the mass market, Japanese language version was released in late 2017. Ring of Fire Press has released a collected edition of his Monster Society stories (set in the New York Times Best-selling world of Eric Flint's 1632). In addition to his fiction, Eric also writes an award-winning comic book news column entitled "Comics in a Flash" as well a pop culture column for Altered Reality Magazine. Eric lives in North Carolina with his wife and two children where he continues to write tales of the hungry dead, blazing guns, and the things that lurk in the woods.

Check out other great
Cryptid Novels!

J.H. Moncrieff
RETURN TO DYATLOV PASS

In 1959, nine Russian students set off on a skiing expedition in the Ural Mountains. Their mutilated bodies were discovered weeks later. Their bizarre and unexplained deaths are one of the most enduring true mysteries of our time. Nearly sixty years later, podcast host Nat McPherson ventures into the same mountains with her team, determined to finally solve the mystery of the Dyatlov Pass incident. Her plans are thwarted on the first night, when two trackers from her group are brutally slaughtered. The team's guide, a superstitious man from a neighboring village, blames the killings on yetis, but no one believes him. As members of Nat's team die one by one, she must figure out if there's a murderer in their midst—or something even worse—before history repeats itself and her group becomes another casualty of the infamous Dead Mountain.

Gerry Griffiths
CRYPTID ZOO

As a child, rare and unusual animals, especially cryptid creatures, always fascinated Carter Wilde. Now that he's an eccentric billionaire and runs the largest conglomerate of high-tech companies all over the world, he can finally achieve his wildest dream of building the most incredible theme park ever conceived on the planet... CRYPTID ZOO. Even though there have been apparent problems with the project, Wilde still decides to send some of his marketing employees and their families on a forced vacation to assess the theme park in preparation for Opening Day. Nick Wells and his family are some of those chosen and are about to embark on what will become the most terror-filled weekend of their lives—praying they survive. STEP RIGHT UP AND GET YOUR FREE PASS... TO CRYPTID ZOO

Check out other great
Cryptid Novels!

Hunter Shea
LOCH NESS REVENGE

Deep in the murky waters of Loch Ness, the creature known as Nessie has returned. Twins Natalie and Austin McQueen watched in horror as their parents were devoured by the world's most infamous lake monster. Two decades later, it's their turn to hunt the legend. But what lurks in the Loch is not what they expected. Nessie is devouring everything in and around the Loch, and it's not alone. Hell has come to the Scottish Highlands. In a fierce battle between man and monster, the world may never be the same. Praise for THEY RISE : "Outrageous, balls to the wall...made me yearn for 3D glasses and a tub of popcorn, extra butter!" – The Eyes of Madness "A fast-paced, gore-heavy splatter fest of sharksploitation." The Werd "A rocket paced horror story. I enjoyed the hell out of this book." Shotgun Logic Reviews

C.G. Mosley
BAKER COUNTY BIGFOOT CHRONICLE

Marie Bledsoe only wants her missing brother Kurt back. She'll stop at nothing to make it happen and, with the help of Kurt's friend Tony, along with Sheriff Ray Cochran, Marie embarks on a terrifying journey deep into the belly of the mysterious Walker Laboratory to find him. However, what she and her companions find lurking in the laboratory basement is beyond comprehension. There are cryptids from the forest being held captive there and something...else. Enjoy this suspenseful tale from the mind of C.G. Mosley, author of Wood Ape. Welcome back to Baker County, a place where monsters do lurk in the night!

Check out other great

Cryptid Novels!

P.K. Hawkins

THE CRYPTID FILES

Fresh out of the academy with top marks, Agent Bradley Tennyson is expecting to have the pick of cases and investigations throughout the country. So he's shocked when instead he is assigned as the new partner to "The Crag," an agent well past his prime. He thinks the assignment is a punishment. It's anything but.Agent George Crag has been doing this job for far longer than most, and he knows what skeletons his bosses have in the closet and where the bodies are buried. He has pretty much free reign to pick his cases, and he knows exactly which one he wants to use to break in his new young partner: the disappearance and murder of a couple of college kids in a remote mountain town.Tennyson doesn't realize it, but Crag is about to introduce him to a world he never believed existed: The Cryptid Files, a world of strange monsters roaming in the night. Because these murders have been going on for a long time, and evidence is mounting that the murderer may just in fact be the legendary Bigfoot.

Gerry Griffiths

DOWN FROM BEAST MOUNTAIN

A beast with a grudge has come down from the mountain to terrorize the townsfolk of Porterville. The once sleepy town is suddenly wide awake. Sheriff Abel McGuire and game warden Grant Tanner frantically investigate one brutal slaying after another as they follow the blood trail they hope will eventually lead to the monstrous killer. But they better hurry and stop the carnage before the census taker has to come out and change the population sign on the edge of town to ZERO.